Y0-BBX-390

GOD OF BEER

GARRET KEIZER

GOD
OF
BEER

HARPERCOLLINSPUBLISHERS

www.harperchildrens.com

Library of Congress Cataloging-in-Publication Data
Keizer, Garret.

God of beer / by Garret Keizer. — 1st ed.

p.   cm.

Summary: To complete a class assignment at his high school in rural Vermont, Kyle and his friends Quake and Diana do a social protest project involving alcohol.

ISBN 0-06-029456-6 — ISBN 0-06-029457-4 (lib. bdg.)

[1. Alcohol—Fiction. 2. Friendship—Fiction. 3. High schools—Fiction. 4. Schools—Fiction.] I. Title.

PZ7.K26 Go 2002   2001024598
[Fic]—dc21   CIP
                                                       AC

Typography by Alison Donalty
1 3 5 7 9 10 8 6 4 2
❖
First Edition

For those I taught,
the living and the dead

GOD OF BEER

Wisdom is vindicated by all her children.

PART 1

1

MY FRIEND QUAKER OATS SAYS THAT I CHANGED HIS LIFE
simply by answering one of Mr. Whalen's questions
in senior social studies class. Maybe I did, and
probably I changed my own life also, though at the
time I had no idea what my friends and I would be
getting into over the next several weeks. To tell you
the truth, I had only the foggiest idea that we
weren't all going to live forever. If I had anything on
my mind that day, it was keeping my eyes off Diana
LaValley's incredible legs.

She was sitting in the desk next to mine, all six
foot four of her, in a majorly short skirt, stockings,
and silver ankle bracelet like the other starters on the
girls' basketball team were wearing because today
they had a game. The boys' version of the dress-up
custom was to put on a tie, maybe with a white shirt
and maybe even with the knot pulled tight, which

was a lot less trouble than the girls took, not to mention a lot less rousing to the old school spirit.

The thing was, though, that Diana and I had been very close friends, never more, for about seven years, and I was determined not to have her catch me gawking at those amazing legs of hers, legs that made her taller than any student, boy or girl, at Willoughby Union, and its girls' team center, and (along with her equally amazing brain) a likely choice for a big scholarship at any one of the eight prestigious schools she'd applied to. Diana always said that I was like a brother to her, and although I wouldn't have minded being more, I would never have done anything to make her see me as less.

So I was just sitting there in class with my shoulders sort of hunched and my eyes straight ahead, something like the way you'd look driving a little foreign beater of a car when an eighteen-wheeler goes roaring by on your left side and you brace yourself on the steering wheel and wait for the powerful afterdraft. Who knows—maybe the expression on my face made me look like I would have some great answer when Mr. Whalen began to ask his question.

"Mahatma Gandhi once said"—Whalen was big on Mahatma Gandhi—"that if God ever came to India, he'd have to come in the form of bread because that is the only way that the starving masses of peasants would be able to understand him."

Whalen was circling the room like he does when he thinks he has an awesome question on his mind or when he's about to take a break from our thematic unit on "Protest Movements of the Twentieth Century" and stroll down memory lane to his early years as a hippie king.

"Now let's for a moment take God as a given, whether or not there actually is a God, and let's take Gandhi's quote and change India to Ira County," that being the part of northern Vermont where I live, along with a lot of deer, moose, and dairy cows. "Or even Willoughby Union High School."

All of a sudden Diana turned and smiled at me, nothing big or sexy but this very kind and steady smile I'd often seen her give to the other girls on her team, especially the younger ones and usually when one of them was stepping up to the foul line. It seemed to say, "Just take your shots, babe, and if they go in, great, and if not, you're great just the same." Looking back now, I wonder if she knew, even before Whalen finished asking his question, that I was the one who was going to answer it.

"So if, according to Gandhi, the only way that God could come to India, the only meaningful way, was as bread, how would God come to . . . let's just make it this school. What form would God have to take if he came to Willoughby Union High?"

I glanced across the room to Quaker Oats, who had started leaning into the question the way he does, with his square chin and his big Adam's apple like a couple of bird dogs' noses in pointing stance. I could imagine him running a billion-gigabyte mental scan of every object and person at Willoughby Union that God might become, not counting Quake himself, who in addition to being the most curious individual I've ever met is also one of the most modest. Everybody else was holding back. Class was almost over. The week was almost over too—five more periods and Friday would start turning into Friday night. God wasn't on the majority of people's minds, I suspect. More likely some party was.

When Whalen repeated the question, we all knew he'd pounce at the end of it. Best now just to wait.

"If God came to India, he'd have to come as bread. If God came to Willoughby Union, he'd have to come as what? Kyle."

That was me. Diana looked at me again with that same encouraging smile.

"Beer," I said.

A couple of kids laughed. Diana's smile went a little crooked.

"Beer?" Whalen was saying. "That's what you said, beer?"

"Beer, yeah."

"Can you explain yourself?" He perched his butt on the empty desk in front of Diana's row. I gave the little shrug guys give to let everybody know that what they're about to say isn't very important to them. Except, with Diana right beside me, it was important.

"I don't know," I said. "It's what people seem the most into. It's what they talk about all the time."

One of the guys in back called out, "That's 'cause there's nothing else to do around here."

"So beer is our bread?" said Whalen.

"I guess."

"But bread is so basic. It keeps people alive. Is beer a thing that keeps you alive?"

A few sillies said yes, one girl said, "Keeps you happy," and the same guy as before said, "There's nothing else to do around here." Diana was turned completely away from me now. That was because Quaker Oats had come to my rescue.

"But we're talking about two different societies," he said. "In India God would have to come as bread because that's all that hungry people can understand, but at this high school God wouldn't *have* to come as anything because all our basic needs are being met. God could come as something basic but it wouldn't have to be something necessary the way it would be

7

in India. Do you see what I mean?"

Whalen looked skeptical, but I think he was mostly trying to process Quake's rapid-fire response. If so, I could sympathize. I've been in that situation more than once myself.

"So you guys are saying that beer . . . is a fundamental motivating force in kids' lives here?"

"Not really," said Jennifer Burch, who likes to give the impression that she handles life as casually as she handles a cigarette or her semiwealthy parents. Nothing is ever a big deal to Jenn; she just "handles it," like breathing, like puking out of an open car door on Saturday night.

"It's just what people do. But like, I agree with Kyle too, because it's just a thing, you know?"

"No, I do not know," Whalen said, teasing her right back.

Jennifer gripped the front of her desk and raised her bottom a few inches off the seat.

"You know," she sang. "It's just . . . Okay." She straightened up all of a sudden and gave her hair a shake. "Bread is like a thing. It's like, it's nothing great, it's nothing bad, it's just a thing."

"An everyday thing, is what she means," said the girl beside her.

"Right, right!" Jennifer said. "Thank you, Cindy." The girls clasped hands as Whalen got off the desk top and moved closer to them.

"So do you have beer every day?" he asked.

Jennifer pointed to herself and said, "Me?" at the same time as some guy behind her said, "I wish."

"There's nothing else to do around here"—one last try from Reggie Barton, who sounded like a guy wondering why nobody else at the bar was paying attention to him.

The bell rang. Whalen called out above the immediate commotion of twenty-six kids breaking camp, "Let's think more about this. We'll visit it again on Monday. Finish the chapter on Gandhi over the weekend."

Quaker Oats caught up with Diana and me just as we were moving through the door.

"Kyle, I think I know what you were getting at." Diana put her arm around him. He was her "brother" too. "And I have an idea," he said, as excited as a little kid.

"You always do, Quake." I said. And it was true. He always did.

2

"SO WHAT'S YOUR IDEA?" I SAID WHEN WE WERE ALL
outside Whalen's class. Quake and Diana would be
taking the nearest stairway down to A.P. physics. I'd
be heading down the hall to get to my locker before
lunch.

"We have to do this term project, which we can
do in teams, right? Let's all do something about
protest and beer. The three of us."

It was a "Quake moment," one of those times
when my friend seemed about to change from matter
into energy right before my eyes. I remember wondering one time when I was a bit buzzed if he was
actually some kind of alien, probably from a planet
more advanced than ours, who'd toddled away from
the mother ship after it landed in Ira County one
night and been found by these two long-haired vege-
tarians, also a ways from home and not too sure what

to do with their beamy little visitor, so they had fed him a carrot, and he was theirs for life.

For us to have been best friends since freshman year, when we first met, is sort of strange, because I am definitely your average down-to-earth earthling, a guy most people couldn't describe without using the word "medium" seven or eight times, as in medium height, medium build, medium smart, medium popular, etc. But then look at Diana, who certainly wasn't medium in any way I could think of. I'd been her close friend as far back as sixth grade, even longer than I'd been friends with Quake.

"You mean like Prohibition?" she was saying, combing her long dark hair with her fingers.

"No. Too much in the past," Quake said. "And anyway, that wasn't really a protest movement. I was thinking more along with Kyle's idea. Beer in the here and now."

I was about to say that Kyle's idea was a bit unclear, not least of all to Kyle, when somebody poked Diana on both sides of her waist and she turned around just in time to see Condor (same as the bird) Christy making his wiseass way down the hall with a big horny grin in her direction. I might have focused another ten seconds of intense dislike on Condor except that I found myself even more focused on the smile Diana was wearing when she turned back around. I'd said "No way" when I first heard the rumor that they had started going out. As one of her closest friends and definitely her closest guy friend, I felt I would know about that before anybody. But I was full of doubt just then, not to mention disgust, which was probably in my voice when I spoke to Quake.

"So what's your idea then? You guys are going to be late."

"Miller doesn't care, as long as we get our labs in. She runs it like college," Diana said. "You shouldn't have dropped it."

"Too much like college," I said.

She squeezed my nose and put her arm around my waist, but that only made me think of Condor's rude fingers jabbing into hers.

"I don't want to study social protest, I want to do it," Quake said. "And Kyle hit the nail right on the head. Beer is the key."

"You don't even drink beer, Quake," I said.

"That's because it's against the law," he said. Diana let go of me and began to tow the law-abiding Quake toward the stairs.

"But what if we were to protest the law? Everybody here thinks the drinking age should be lower than twenty-one."

"Yeah," I called just as he was about to walk

through the fire door Diana was holding open for him, "but everybody here drinks just the same."

"You're going to the game, right?"

"He better," Diana said.

"Come to my house after school," Quake said. "We'll talk about it there. Then we'll go watch the Goddess Diana triumph over her mortal adversaries."

I held up two fingers of my one hand against the index finger of the other to make a K, as in one thousand, the number of career points Diana was almost guaranteed to have racked up by the first quarter of tonight's game.

The halls were almost clear by the time I had lunch out of my locker. No sooner had I banged the door shut than I noticed what looked like the beginning of a rumble outside the resource room.

Standing in the doorway, at two hundred plus pounds and twenty-one years of age (though nobody's supposed to know that), in red-flannel shirt, stained blue jeans, and high-top logger boots, the King of the Resource Room, Mrs. Cantor's favorite if also most exasperating pupil, and occasional hunting and fishing partner of yours truly, David "Mountain Man" Logan. I could tell he was really pissed, because above his two days' growth of reddish beard his face was redder still.

Facing Mr. Logan, eye level to the redneck's neck so to speak, at something like one hundred and sixty pounds, most of it chiseled muscle, in the ponytail that was supposed to identify him as an artist, and the baggy hundred-dollar sweater that was supposed to identify him as a prep, and the saggy black pants and basketball sneakers that were supposed to identify him as the undisputed expert on everything that black boys do (though he be a very white boy himself, but a white boy who'd lived in the most happening state of California till his school kicked him out), the man of a thousand endowments, Condor Christy— a.k.a. C.C., Big Bird, Rubberman, This Real Cute Guy, This Major Horse's Ass, though on a superficial level he and I get along okay.

The shoving hadn't gotten ugly yet, but serious enough for the less brawny inhabitants of the resource room to have backed a few feet inside it and for Mrs. Cantor to be calling, "David, come inside."

"What's up?" I said when I got closer.

"He's being smart," David said, giving a good shove to Condor's shoulder.

"Hey, Kyle." Condor gave me a thumb-over-thumb handshake while holding out his other hand against David's chest. "I'm being smart."

"Boys!" Mrs. Cantor's face was in the doorway, trying its sweet best to look stern. "David, come inside. And you get to class, young man."

"Mrs. Cantor wants you, Davy," Condor said.

I'm not sure he was aware of his own danger. David comes off slow and sluggish in a lot of ways, but he has a wicked bad temper, he's extremely strong, and he can sometimes move faster than most of us can think. I've seen him shoulder a rifle so fast I never even saw it move—I just saw it in one position, and then I saw it in another. Then again he usually can't do a *series* of things fast, which meant that if David's first punch didn't kill him, Condor might be able to beat him in a fight, not without getting hurt himself, though.

"You think you're smart," David said again. I noticed he'd clenched his right hand.

"No, but some people do. Some people think I'm real smart."

"That's what you are."

"David, come inside now. Class is beginning," Mrs. Cantor pleaded.

"Anybody think you're smart, David?"

Condor backed away from the shove he knew was coming in reply and started down the hall even before David had regained his balance. Mrs. Cantor put her hand on David's shoulder and again said, "Come inside."

"That guy's heading for trouble," David said to

me, his chest heaving. "He don't know it, but he's heading for trouble."

"Let's let him head there all by himself. Mrs. Cantor, you mind if I have some of my lunch in here?"

"No, Kyle, I certainly do not." I knew she wouldn't. Anyway, that's how we got David back into the resource room.

3

DAVID WOULDN'T EVEN TALK TO ME AT FIRST, BUT THAT'S
just his way. When he's mad, he's mad at the world.
In that case it's best to stay close without crowding
him and wait for him to come around, which he will
usually do as if nothing had bothered him in the first
place.

So after David had slammed his books down on a
desk near the windows, and while he gave Mrs.
Cantor a few grumpy nods as she tried to talk to him,
I took the unoccupied seat next to her desk and got to
work on a ham-and-cheese sandwich. Mrs. Cantor
usually keeps a few sodas in a little fridge on the
floor. I grabbed one of these, dropping all the change
I had in my pocket into the donation can. A light
snow was falling outside, nothing unusual for
February but bound to help David improve his mood,
since fresh snow means easy tracking and guarantees

another day's snowmobiling on the tail end of winter. To tell you the truth, I didn't mind shooting the breeze with Mrs. Cantor for a few minutes till David calmed down. She's one of the few teachers in that school who aren't always giving me a pain by asking about my future. Plus I usually get a kick out of her. Quake does too.

First of all, she's so incredibly calm and gentle that it's almost funny. In the privacy of our own homes Quake and I used to do these hilarious impersonations of Mrs. Cantor in various panic scenarios, like "I'd probably put those salt and pepper shakers away now, David, because we're about to be visited by dribbling cannibal psychopaths and we wouldn't want to tease those fellows. Of course, if they're very hungry, I do have this left arm that I don't use all that much."

Also, Mrs. Cantor is incredibly smart for someone who teaches slow kids. I suppose we shouldn't be so surprised by that, but like a lot of people, my friends and I tend to think that teachers are intelligent according to the grade or ability of their students (although my mom dated a college teacher once who claimed it usually works the other way around. After a month of going out with him, my mom agreed). Anyway, whenever Mrs. Cantor asks what you're studying, and no matter what it is, she almost always has something intelligent to say about it. One time Quake and I made up something totally bogus—the strange courtship rituals of the Wahwah people, or something along those lines—just to see if Mrs. Cantor was really as smart as she seemed or just an incredible b.s. artist. We've always been a little ashamed of testing her like that.

"I guess I'm drawing a blank on that one," she said. We kept pretty good poker faces till she looked out the window and sighed. "You fellows wouldn't be pulling my leg, would you?"

We never tried to fool her like that again.

Of course, like any teacher past a certain age—I would put her somewhere between thirty-five and fifty—she has peculiar ideas that belong to an older way of thinking. She asked if I was doing anything interesting in class these days, and I mentioned the protest unit and the term project, though I wasn't about to say anything about beer, even when she asked what I was planning to do.

"I guess a lot of the kids are going to do something from the Sixties because Whalen's all into that, and also because of the music scene back then."

"Is anybody going to do something about the early labor struggles?" she asked. "It's a very interesting part of history, and it's very relevant to some matters right here in our own backyard."

I listened politely as she went on about this and that factory going on strike, but it all sounded pretty boring to me. All I could imagine was my father and the other jugheads locked out of the Salmon Falls jug mill during "the famous jug mill strike of 1893," at which point I could also imagine them dropping their picket signs and all heading over to the Salmon Taps for a couple of cold pitchers apiece. Here's to the strike. Half an hour later it'd be like, What strike? Mrs. Cantor seemed completely fascinated, though. Then again, I've heard some of her music, which no one my age except Quaker Oats could ever find appealing, and he'll listen to anything. Maybe when you're an exceptionally mellow person like Mrs. Cantor, you need to think about commotions that are fairly old-fashioned and not too rowdy. It might be all your nerves can take. How else can you explain her telling me that a bunch of women walking away from their sewing machines in nineteen-o-something was "a hundred times more radical than Woodstock"?

I don't see it.

Fortunately David waved me over to the windows before I had to say too much about early labor struggles, though I did thank Mrs. Cantor for her suggestions.

"Hey, dude, what you doing?" This is David's usual greeting, but only here in the resource room, or when the two of us are by ourselves.

"Eating my lunch, dude," I said, pulling a desk close to his. "Want half an orange?"

"Don't mind if I do, don't mind if I don't." I peeled a seam and tore the fruit in two. I gave him the bigger half.

"So you going to see the girls play tonight?" I asked with my mouth juicy-full of orange. "Tonight's probably going to be when Diana gets her thousandth point."

Dave considered that, also chewing.

"She's a nice girl. Real pretty, too. Maybe I'll go, maybe I won't. I have to check, see if my father needs me."

That was a subject I didn't want to get too close to, any more than I wanted to pry into the reason for the pushing match before. No need really. Condor was a jerk, and for that matter, as nearly as I could tell, so was David's dad. The only difference was that Condor was the up-and-coming variety, whereas Mr. Logan was more the caveman variety.

"What about the party Saturday night?" David said. "The Burch girl's. That Jennifer."

I was surprised. I couldn't believe Jennifer had invited David, who isn't always acceptable even at some of the redneck parties. So-called rednecks can be extremely sensitive about people who might tarnish the redneck image, that is, people like David Logan, who don't know how to act like rednecks mainly because they *are* rednecks.

But I wasn't any better than those guys—for just a minute I was afraid David was going to ask me to take him along to Jennifer's. I said I wasn't sure if I'd go, which was a lie.

"I might go to that one," he said.

"Great."

"Probably Diana'll be there, too."

"Probably—"

"Which case that Condor'll be there also, I suppose."

"Not necessarily," I said. "Why would he?"

"Oh, he likes her."

"Well . . . maybe she likes him too," I said, probably hoping that if I admitted as much, then it wouldn't be true.

"No way, dude. She's too smart for that. Diana's wicked smart. He only thinks he's smart. But his kind of smart's the kind I don't like."

"What you doing here?" I asked, nodding toward his book.

"Math," he said, spitting out the word. "Someday, if I ever get set up, I tell you what." I'd heard this a hundred times. "No more math, no more crap from anybody, and no more scrounging around for my old man."

"Want some help?"

"Maybe I do, maybe I don't."

I tried to play it cool. "Well," I said, stretching my arms over my head, "I got ten more minutes before lunch is over."

He had no reason not to let me help. For every minute we'd ever spent together on his homework, we'd spent three hours in the woods, and in that classroom David was the tutor and I was the one getting the extra help. That's how it was with all my best friends. Each of them was good at something special (they were all taller than me too)—Diana at basketball and Dave in the woods and Quake at being an all-round genius. My only claim to any special talent was that I could be good friends with all three.

4

ONE OF QUAKE'S FAVORITE JOKES ABOUT HIMSELF IS
that because he never learned to fight, he had to learn
to run. By the time we got to know each other, there
weren't many bullies on two legs who could have
caught him. He goes out for track and cross-country,
which is partly how he came to know Diana, and he
holds the school records for the cross-country course
and the mile. But as great as he is to watch going
around a track or smoking down a cross-country
path, where he is truly awesome is tearing through
the deep woods or playing tag Frisbee in a cow pas-
ture with his shirt off and his hair blowing and his
long lean body in perfect sync with the terrain, duck-
ing branches or dodging cow pies—or, like he was
that Friday after school coming toward me over
the rise where his house sits, deliberately plow-
ing through the deepest snow, a bit clumsy as you

couldn't help but be in a two-and-a-half-foot snow-pack, but absolutely unstoppable, rearing up like a horse with wild wolves in pursuit, or like this wiry extraterrestrial who's grown up on earth but can still remember his old planet, where they also have plenty of snow.

He was leaning over with both hands on his knees when I got out of my car.

"Looks like you're a little out of shape there, Quake."

He straightened up and grinned, still puffing. "Race you back to the shed."

"Nah. I got to rest up from getting out of the car."

I looked out across the valley at the snow-covered farms and frozen ponds, then down at the metal roofs and white steeples of Schumansville, tucked at the foot of Quake's mountain. It was a beautiful sight—I could see why his parents had chosen this spot to set up their teepee and start building their house just before their son appeared. I guess they were something like hippies back then, or their own version anyway, heavy on the peace and love, light on the guns and ganja. Extra light on the guns. Quake's family are members of the Quaker religion, which means they do not believe in violence of any kind, not even in self-defense. So Quake was, you might say, born to run.

You would think that when people found out you weren't going to fight back, no matter how hard they pushed you or what names they called you, that would be the end of it as far as violence goes, but that's not how it had worked for Quake. It's not like he got the crap knocked out of him every day after school—he says that only happened a couple of times—it was more little stuff, like being pushed from behind at the water fountain or getting squeezed into a locker or being called a faggot or a pussy because people know they're not going to get anything back for it like a fully loaded cafeteria tray in the face, which is how I put a stop to an eighth grader who was doing similar stuff to me when I was in sixth. Not that I would consider myself the violent type—this happened around the time when my parents were splitting up, when it didn't take much to get me mad. Still, I notice that sometimes I can't resist bringing up violent stuff around Quake. It isn't something I especially like about myself.

"Condor Christy almost found out if there was an afterlife this noon," I said as we trudged toward the woodshed. I gave him the blow-by-blow of Condor's confrontation with David Logan.

"David should just ignore somebody like that," Quake said. "Do you know what it was about?"

"No, I don't. But I think old Dave may be on the

warpath. He was talking about going to the party at Jennifer's on Saturday, which I can't believe he was invited to, but he seemed pretty keen on knowing whether Condor would be there."

"Is Condor going out with Diana?"

"I don't know. She hasn't said anything about it to me."

"Me neither."

"So why did you ask if they were going out?"

Quake merely shrugged his shoulders. "Want to throw a couple snakes?"

I said, "Sure," though I really wanted to see if Quake knew any more than I did about Condor and Diana. Snakes is a winter game the Iroquois Indians used to play, where you whip these shaved, six-foot poles over a track of packed-down snow to see whose "snake" goes farther. Quake says the Iroquois used hickory sticks with lead tips; his are maple with hammered-on points made from old haymow teeth. Snakes is one of about a dozen play-around things his family does instead of watching TV.

"Could David be jealous?" I said, after my snake had come rattling to a halt a few yards behind his. "Do you think he likes her?"

"I think most of the straight guys at school like her." That took me back a little, because as far as that goes, Quake is straight too. Right away he ran off to retrieve our snakes and came roaring back to change the subject.

"But I don't think that's why they're fighting," he said. "Condor gives David the needle sometimes. I hear him say things about him in art class that aren't too complimentary."

"I could say some things about his so-called art that aren't too complimentary."

"You can throw these some more, if you want," Quake offered. "I have to finish splitting wood for the kitchen stove."

Of course I went to help Quake. Inside the shed I took up the ax as he leaned the snakes against a corner.

"Condor's actually pretty good at drawing," Quake offered, throwing a half chunk of maple on the block. We'd take turns with the ax till there was an armful for each of us.

"All his drawings are the same crap," I said, timing the word "crap" so it came out at the same time as my blade cracked the wood. "All these muscle-bound superhero types. You know what I think? I think he's drawing himself—the way he imagines himself. His favorite subject."

"Condor's just insecure." Quake took the ax from me and finished the piece. I lugged another from the pile and set it up.

"So what's he got against David? Is David too secure for him? Too cocky about being in the resource room half the day trying to pass his frigging math course?"

"David's what Condor hates about living here. He's going to this big school in California where everybody wears the latest clothes and half the kids are driving a BMW or a Mercedes, and then all of a sudden he gets in some kind of trouble and his parents move him way up here and he feels like he's been exiled to hickland. David is like everything he resents about living in the sticks walking toward him on two legs."

"Yeah, well, he ought to go back where he came from." I struck the wood so hard that the ax stuck in the chopping block. "Pack up his resentment and vamoose. David's worth a dozen of him any day."

"David's great. But you can't really reach him either, you know? It's like what you said in class today about beer. I've been thinking about that all day. If Gandhi—or like Mr. Whalen was saying, God—came here, how would they talk to somebody like David and his friends? How could they make themselves as easy to understand as bread would be to a hungry peasant? You were right. They'd have to use beer."

We both had an armload now. I helped him steady

the piece he was trying to hold under his chin.

"I was just joking, Quake. You realize that, don't you?"

"But it isn't a joke. Drinking is like a religion around here. It really is. People live for it. Some people die for it. Literally."

"You're not going to stop people from drinking," I said, following him toward the house. "You couldn't stop me."

"I wouldn't want to. But could a small group of people, like us, like you and me and Diana, and maybe David and even Condor—"

"David wouldn't go near it, and forget Condor."

"Could they stop people, not from drinking, but from being so obsessive and hypocritical about it? The way it is now, parents tell their kids not to drink but know they'll drink anyway, kids feel they have to drink even when they don't want to drink, and all anybody seems to talk about is how much they drank last weekend—it's not like that in a lot of other cultures, you know."

"Yeah, but this is this culture."

We were in the kitchen now, warm and full of spicy smells. We dropped the wood into the box next to the black cookstove.

"Culture can be changed. In India they had people called untouchables—"

"Because you weren't even supposed to touch them. I know."

"You weren't even supposed to let their *shadow* touch you, that's how low class they were considered, and that was *their* culture, and Gandhi knew he had to change it. So if beer is our culture, we can change that too. That's our project, Kyle. I don't know the details yet, but that's our project."

I looked at him closely—he had his classic Quake face on.

"So how's this going to work then? You're going to be Gandhi"—he protested, of course—"nope, you're going to be Gandhi, and God's going to be beer, and David's going to be one of the hungry peasants—"

"He'll drink the beer."

"Right." He still had that goofy grin of his, and I was probably wearing one just like it. "And what about me? What am I, Quake?"

"You're the one who saw the light! You are, Kyle. You're the Buddha boy."

He was embarrassing me.

"Well . . . right now the Buddha boy should go see his mother. Before she has a sacred cow. Then let's go see the Lady Di."

"The Huntress."

"The Tall One."

"LaValley from the Valley."

The next thing came into my mouth before it made any sense in my head.

"The untouchable."

5

QUAKE'S MOM TOLD ME I COULD STAY FOR SUPPER, which she always does when I'm over to his house, but today I had to head home. One of my mom's "house rules" is that there can be no day when we're both in town that we don't eat at least one meal together. Sometimes I complain about that rule, and it can be a pain sometimes, but I never don't respect the fact that I have a mother who wants to spend time with me.

I guess that's one of the ways my mom and Quake's are alike, another being that they are both beautiful women, not only as in pretty, which they both definitely are, but beautiful in the way they treat other people and bring up their kids. They're different in a lot of ways too. His is in her forties and has as much gray hair as blond, which she wears long, and went to college and runs a small catalog business out of her house selling clothes and blankets that she and her friends sew and weave, while my mom had me right after high school so she didn't go to college and is still pretty young even now. Her hair is dark brown and short, she smokes (though she's tried a few times to quit), and she's a bookkeeper at Northeast Plastics, the jug mill where my father works on the line. There's the other big difference: Quake's mother has always seemed unbelievably in love with his dad, whereas my parents split when I was about eleven for reasons I don't completely understand but that definitely had something to do with my dad drinking too much or my mom thinking that he did and definitely had nothing to do—so they say—with me.

My mom still goes out with guys—in fact, she goes out a lot more than I do, which sometimes feels embarrassing for the two of us. Not that her boyfriends are ever in my face. Another of Mom's house rules is nobody sleeps in the house except her and me, or once in a while a guy friend of mine who's expected to follow the other house rules that apply to him such as no yelling in the house, no F-word in the house, no booze in the house (though Mom knows I drink when I go out, and I know she does too), and no clothes on the floor, dirty or clean. She still does most of my laundry, though, and she's never given me that "When you're eighteen" bit as in "When I can finally boot your ass out." In fact, I turned eighteen last November, and she told me that same day, "You'll always have a home here."

Anyway, that's where I was heading after I left Quake's house in the woods. I wound my way to the interstate, where one exit down I'd be in Salmon Falls. The whole drive back I was wondering to myself how we were going to turn beer into a social studies project and wishing Quake and I had spent more time talking about it. I didn't mind going home, though. One difference between Quake and me is that he doesn't really live anywhere except his own wild imagination, and if he does ever find himself living someplace real someday, it definitely won't be in the boonies of Schumansville (though it might be in the boonies of Antarctica or New Guinea).

Myself, on the other hand, I live in Salmon Falls, I've hung out on every street in that town, I've probably run through half the backyards at one time or another at different hours of the night, and I wouldn't be at all surprised if in fifty years I'm one of the toothless old geezers sitting out in front of the hotel drinking coffee in the morning and winking at the women on their way to the mill. Sometimes people say to me—even my friends will say to me, "Won't it bother you to be stuck here and to wonder if you could have done something better?" And I'll say, "Won't it bother you to be stuck someplace else that turns out to be no better than here, maybe worse, and to wonder if *you* could have done something better, because everybody wonders that no matter what they do?" Or I'll say, "Won't it bother you to wonder if the only reason you left town was because all your friends did the same thing?" Probably it won't, though. Probably they'll be doing just fine, probably a lot better than I will. But whatever things are bothering me twenty years from now, I bet one of them won't be that I live in Salmon Falls. I even like the stupid things about this town, like the very funky Christmas lights they string across Railroad Street, which remind me of the dimmer lights at the fairground, which I also like. And I like the humming of the mill and the little hydraulic hisses you can hear in the night when the injection molds open up to drop a set of jugs, and even the way the public library ended up somehow on top of the firehouse, where they say the cracks in the second-floor ceiling were made by the heads of librarians jumping out of their chairs every time the fire whistle went off.

Once I get off the interstate, I like to take the long way home, which goes around the far shore of Salmon Pond and the series of short waterfalls that gave the town its name. There's a small wooded island in the center of the pond—now and then you'll see a picture of it on a calendar or a postcard. And there you have another interesting thing about Salmon Falls and some of the other towns around here too, which were also built next to lakes or ponds, and that's the way that the old-timers seem to have laid out the town, and especially the main street, so that no one would ever have to look at the water. It's almost like they were afraid that in a place where most people have to bust their butts every day just to stay off welfare, looking at anything too beautiful might make them forget to go to work. So they had to turn their backs, or at least the backs of their buildings, on the scenery. That's my theory anyway, and Quake says it's pretty awesome. I know this old artist who lives in town, and when I told my theory to him, he said that most people are probably afraid that too much beauty will make them weak. I've never had that fear myself, and I think my mother is probably one of the main reasons.

Mom has always had a soft spot in her heart for Dave Logan and the kind of low-grade anxiety about Quake that you'd expect her to have about David. She was true to form when I told her the day's events as we helped ourselves to the casserole she'd put together after work.

"This Condor character sounds like a big creep."

"He is," I said, but real low key.

"Who'd be so stupid as to pick on Dave? First of all he could break you in two. And he's just a big old lug with a heart the size of Michigan. Jeez'um crow. But I've seen the same garbage at work."

"Good food, Mom."

"Thanks, hon. Eat up. I don't want it left over."

I was a little unspecific about our social studies project, especially since Quake and I hadn't gotten all that specific about it ourselves, but I did mention that it might have something to do with drinking.

"I don't get it," Mom said.

"I don't really get it either. But I think between the three of us, Quake, Diana, and me, we're going to come up with something that's different, you know. Not the same old report. Something that'll make people stop and think."

"Just be careful, okay? It's your senior year. Just get through it and try to enjoy it. Don't let your smarty-pants friends get you mixed up in something that turns out to be more trouble than it's worth."

I was ready for my second helping. She was done, as usual. She always says she'd rather watch me eat than eat herself.

"What you got against Quake?" I said.

"Nothing, honey," she said, coughing. "I love

Quake." She was trying to clear her throat. "He's sweet, he's brilliant. Someday, I have every confidence, he's going to be a world-famous scientist or something like that—if he doesn't wind up in the loony bin." She held her hands on either side of her head and made them shake. "He's always thinking. You have to give it a rest once in a while. That boy needs a girlfriend."

"Condor Christy may have a new girlfriend," I said. "The guy who was hassling David. You'll never guess who."

"Somebody I know, I assume."

She got up from the table and cracked the window over the sink a couple of inches. She took her purse off the coat tree by the door.

"I'm going to have just a few puffs, that's all, I swear. It's too cold to go outside."

I made it a point to say nothing. "So who's the girl?" She stood by the sink with one arm folded in front of her and the other cocked beside her, holding the lit cigarette next to her ear. I wished I hadn't brought this up.

"Diana LaValley. It's just a rumor. I can't believe she'd go out with an idiot like that."

Now it was Mom who wasn't answering, though she was wearing her best know-it-all smile.

"You got to quit that," I said, taking my plate

over to the sink. She fanned the air in front of her.

"I know. I know. I'm going to quit soon, I swear."

"You're killing yourself."

"I know, jeez'um. It calms my nerves. Someday when you have a teenager you'll appreciate that."

We were facing each other now, each leaning against a different edge of countertop.

"Look, instead of talking about my health, let's talk about your love life."

"Get out of here."

"When are you going to ask her out?"

"Ask who?"

"Diana LaValley. Who else?"

"What for?"

"You love her, Kyle. You've loved her for years."

I fanned the smoke away from my face, pretending it annoyed me.

"You've carried a torch for her so long you're about to burn your fingers."

"It's not like that, okay? You . . ." I shook my head, the why-bother motion. She touched my arm. "We're friends. We're like brother and sister. Diana is my sister."

"Says who? I don't remember giving birth to any babies named Diana. This brother-and-sister routine ain't your idea. That's Diana's idea."

"So what if it is? It's what we are to each other."

She took one more deep drag on her cigarette before stubbing it out. "You want to know something about women?" she said, turning to exhale toward the window crack.

"They get lung cancer just like men?" That was cruel. "Look, I'm sorry. Tell me something about women."

"Listen, Kyle, I don't give jackshit who you go out with. I don't care if you go out at all. I'm your mother, I love you, and I just want you to have some of the things you want. The things *you* want, okay? Not me. It isn't my life."

"Tell me something about women."

We locked eyes for a minute, and then her face grew softer. I already knew at least one thing about women: The one in this kitchen couldn't stay mad at me if she tried.

"Listen up. You'll thank me for this someday."

"I'll thank you now in case I forget. Thank you."

"You know what a harem is, right? Well, if women ever kept harems, they'd be different from men's harems. A man's harem has all different kinds of women but they're all there for the same reason, basically."

"What reason's that?"

"Yeah—you're in bad shape, but you ain't in that bad a shape. Anyway, in a woman's harem only some of the men would be lovers, maybe only one. The others would be like good friends, or some would be best friends, and some would be good advice-givers, and a couple would be all-around hell-raisers just for the fun of it. Women are like moviemakers, Kyle—they have a part for every guy in their lives. They write the script. And they have every right in the world to do that because it's their life. But you know what guys have every right to do? Guys have every right to say, 'I read your script, honey, and I don't like my part. You got me down for the brother part? I think I'd be real good in the boyfriend part. I think you should let me try out for that part.'"

"Would you like to tell her all this? Would that make you happy?" I didn't say it in a nasty way.

"It's what makes *you* happy! Sure, I'll tell her. I'll call her up right now."

"Put the phone down, Mom." She held it to her ear without dialing.

"Hello, Diana. My son, Kyle, is a little shy, except when he's mouthing off to his mother, but he's positively dying for you, and if you don't agree to go out with him at least once, I'm worried he'll be so upset he's going to go off on a bender with Quaker Oats and try to get social studies credit for it."

"Very funny." She seemed to think so. I took the phone out of her hand and kissed her cheek.

"I'll be home after the game."

"What do you have to lose?" she called after me.

"Her friendship."

"That's one thing you never have to be afraid of losing, honey. If it's real, it don't get lost."

6

DIANA ONLY NEEDED SEVEN POINTS TO MAKE THE thousandth of her high school career. A lot of people in the gym that night expected her to score them in the first fifteen minutes or so of the game, but Wheeler Mountain had a good team, they were long-time rivals of Willoughby Union, and they seemed every bit as intent on keeping Diana from her glory points as on winning the game—not that there was much of a difference between those two objectives.

We were ahead twelve to ten after about twenty minutes, but Diana had only scored four. Beyond the fact of double coverage, which was almost a given for Diana these days, she didn't seem at her best. She was missing too many shots, though no shot she took was easy. If I believed in luck, I'd have said hers wasn't with her. What I wanted to believe was that Condor Christy was throwing her off, sitting up high in the bleachers with his fan club and booming this "Dian-UH" every two minutes. To my way of thinking it would be the perfect Condoresque maneuver to make a big display of rooting for Diana while secretly hoping to mess her up.

He'd made his entrance about five minutes after the game started, all pumped up from lifting in the weight room, where he likes to go after wrestling practice. The school board wasn't spending any extra money to heat the gym in February, but of course he had on a tight T-shirt so you could appreciate all the details. He'd showered so that his blondish hair looked darker and his wet ponytail looked more like a muskrat tail. Passing in front of where David and Quake were sitting on either side of me, he gave this very dignified nod and said, "Ladies."

"Must be he can't tell girls from boys," David said after Condor had passed to the higher bleachers. "There's a word for guys like that."

"But we're not going to say it, right?"

"Whoa!" Quake cried. Diana had just missed a beautiful outside shot. It seemed from where we sat that it should have gone in. That's when Condor started his Dian-UH bit.

I'm sure it was him too that sang out in a deep voice, followed by squeals of high-pitched laughter and a few ape chortles from the unfairer sex: "'Davy,

Davy Crockett, king of the wild frontier.'"

"What's that retard saying now?" David said. He turned around and was about to stand up when Quake leaned over me and said, "Dave. Dave. It's not about you. It's from an old television show. It's on cable now."

I looked directly at Quake after David had hunkered down again. "Really. I thought you didn't watch television."

"Yeah, but this is *classic* television. Trivia test: Who played Davy Crockett in the television series of that name?"

"Quake—"

"Fess Parker."

"Quake, number one, you're my favorite Martian. Number two, I don't give a flying. All right?"

"Dian-UH!" Condor bellowed from above. Something had just happened on the court, but I'd missed what it was. When I turned to ask David what I hadn't seen, we heard that mock-bass singing again.

"'Killt him a b'ar when he was only three.'"

My mom didn't need to worry about Quake or any other high school kid landing in the loony bin. We'd already landed.

• • •

Watching Diana make her foul shots that night, or any night, was like going to mass or a bullfight or some other ceremony where a person stands up straight and makes these very formal motions in front of something big and awesome that has the power to kill him. (If you say "It's only a basketball game, for Pete's sake," you've never gone to a basketball game in Ira County.) Diana always stood up straight—she was not one of these tall girls who give their breasts a complex on account of their height. But out on the court, towering above the other players and refs, she looked even taller than usual. She told me once that most of her people were French or Scottish but that somewhere back in her family tree there were a few Montagnais Indians, who were known to be tall suckers, and I don't doubt it. The Willoughby girls' sleeveless uniforms, white with red lettering, made her jet-black hair and olive skin stand out. She dribbled the ball several times, raising her head to look at the basket after she caught the last bounce. Then, with the ball held firmly between her hands, which were small, really, compared to the rest of her, she extended her arms away from her body, still bent at the elbows but so far out that if they belonged to a man-made structure instead of a human body, you'd worry that the span was too great

and the whole thing might collapse. It was just amazing to see her hold something that far out from herself—with bent arms besides—and still be holding it.
If she ever had a baby, she could make him feel like
he was in a whole other orbit from his mother, but
still held by her gravity—a nice feeling as I imagined
it. Then her forearms cocked back, but watch the ball
now—and *swish*.

One more, Diana. Luck can't hurt you now.

The crowd held its breath as she took the ball
again, bowing her head a second time and letting one
of her legs relax so that her knee nudged forward.
Dribble, stretch, shoot—how long could you watch
that kind of perfection before it got boring? A long
time, I think.

But it wouldn't be the perfect shot itself, or the
thrill of seeing someone score her thousandth point, or
even how beautiful a girl she was that held your attention, although they'd be good reasons. It would be
something in the way she raised her head and always
brought that wayward knee back into line and
pumped that ball against the boards of the hushed
gym like a heartbeat that made you suddenly realize
that she was sacrificing some of her life every time
that ball went through the hoop, which she was, and
which we all are with every single thing we do, but

watching Diana take her foul shots could make you see it for the very first time.

When the game was over, Diana had managed to score twenty-one points over her thousand, which beat the school record by three and put her within striking distance of the record set for the whole league. It would take her an hour to get off the court. Even the girls from the other team threw their arms around her neck, and some of them cried. When she saw me in the crowd, she ratcheted those amazing arms of hers right between a couple of other heads and took mine in her hands like a basketball. The look on her face—I'll tell you, being her brother wasn't such a bad thing right then. And do girls usually kiss their brothers on the mouth?

"You're the greatest," I told her. "I'm so proud of you."

It was one of those times when you feel you're in the perfect place. My best friends were on either side of me, and she was in front of me, and everybody else was there just to press us together. Some kids behind us were chanting, "Lady Di! Lady Di!"

Most of the crowd had melted back by the time this great red torch of roses suddenly appeared in front of her. I watched her expression change to something I wasn't sure I'd ever seen on her face, just before I turned to see Condor offering the bouquet.

She smelled it, clutched it to her breast, did all the things that women are supposed to do with a big bunch of roses, and then handed them to one of her teammates while she gave Condor his first delicious reward.

I had meant to offer her a ride home, but I couldn't do that now. Sure enough, Condor turned to me, and in that fake deep voice of his, he said, "I'll see your sister is home by eleven, Kyle."

Had she actually told him I was her pretend brother?

Then in that same ridiculous voice he said his good-byes to Quake and Dave, nodding to each one.

"Mistuh Oats. Mistuh Crockett."

He walked Diana to the door of the girls' locker room with his arm around her waist. I heard David say, "That guy thinks he's smart."

"No, David," I snapped. "That guy don't *think* he's smart. He *is* smart."

7

WHEN DIANA CALLED ME UP SATURDAY MORNING AND asked for a ride to Jenn Burch's party that night, I was shocked into instant happiness—the shock I live for. It's not like it was unusual for her to ride with me to a party or anywhere else. It was just that after the night before, I was assuming that she'd ride there with C.C. if anybody. It was on the tip of my tongue to say so, but I was smart enough not to bring him up. She asked if I could give her friend Shannon a ride too. No problem.

When I got to the LaValley farm, they were standing outside together, blowing cold breath in the light streaming off the porch. Diana got in back, which was not my preference for a seating arrangement, but the car was small enough that it wasn't much different than if she'd sat in front. Plus I liked Shannon all right. She could be a little silly at times, but it was a sweet kind of silly, and there are days when having somebody like Shannon in your car is a better idea than a first-aid kit. She also had a crush on Quake, which tickled me for some reason.

"The rip in your ceiling's a lot bigger," Diana said from behind me.

"One of Quake's skis snagged it."

"Does he ski?" Shannon asked.

"Oh yeah," I said. "He does everything."

The thing I always liked about giving a ride to Diana, especially when another person was along, was the way she always made some comment about my car that referred to another time she'd been in it, like "You still haven't thrown away this candy wrapper" or "When did you move the station?" It was like she was saying for my benefit and anybody else's in the car, "We're good friends."

What if Condor wasn't coming to the party at all? Another dose of instant happiness might be on its way.

Jennifer Burch's A-frame was in a nice spot, backed into the slope of a small hill with a view of Mount Zion and a wide deck on three sides, although with the temperature now hovering around zero, I doubted many people would be on it long unless Jenn made a stink about people smoking in the house. Her parents would not be there, but people would more or less do what Jenn said, because she had that knack of making you do what she wanted, which, let's face it, some individuals have and some don't.

Sometime around last Christmas a sophomore named Maureen Young had invited a lot of juniors and seniors to a party that people later said went sour mainly because Maureen was too stuck up about her connections to upperclassmen. I wasn't there, but from what I heard, things got rowdy when Condor and a few other guys started putting on a pro-wrestling-type exhibition that took out a lamp or two as well as a couple of the weaker chairs. After that it was go wild or go home, and nobody wanted to go home, even though by this time Maureen was practically hysterical yelling at everybody to stop it. I guess the house was pretty much trashed. That would never happen to Jennifer Burch, although her parents could certainly afford the damage better than Maureen's. The A-frame wasn't even the Burches' regular house, just a camp.

There were quite a few vehicles in the dooryard when we got there, so I parked on the drive as far over as I could get without sinking a tire in deep snow, and we walked to the A-frame with the plowed surface creaking underfoot. We could hear the dull throb of bass chords coming from inside the house and see the silhouettes of our friends moving in candlelight across the ceiling. A stream of thick white wood smoke rose straight up from the chimney. Shannon began to jog up the drive, holding her mittens over her ears. Diana patted my back and jogged off after her. I took the pat to mean that I didn't have to run.

I walk fast, though, so I was in the door almost as soon as they were. I was met by that triple body slam of loud music, hot air, and the jolt you never quite get over from your first real party, maybe in sixth or seventh grade, of seeing all your daylight classmates in their vampire mode, altar boys passing a J and the class president on her boyfriend's lap with her legs a bit loose and her skirt riding high—half the National Honor Society with its ceremonial white candles turned to brown bottles of beer. To tell you the truth, it always gives me a charge. It's like those sci-fi movies where the aliens peel off their skin to show their real faces or like any good-size town in any place but the boonies when night comes and the lights come on, like it is on the midway of the Ira County Fair after the little kids go home. I wonder if people get drunk to make that dark woozy feeling come over them or because they wouldn't know how to face it otherwise.

People were still cheering from when Diana had stepped through the door. Though the party had been planned for a couple of weeks, it had sort of become a celebration of her thousandth point. There was even a banner to that effect hanging on one of the walls. Jennifer came over to kiss us and to shout over the music how glad she was we came. Condor was right behind her, looking a bit buzzed already when he took my hand and did his homeboy handshake. Newer arrivals were stomping snow off their feet behind us, and it was time to scatter and find our own drinks and company.

I stepped over the legs of people sitting on the floor, saying hi as I went, and took the first beer held out to me. I looked around for David, but just as I suspected, he hadn't come. I was sure he hadn't been invited either. Often David's big thing is to act like he might do, or else refuses to do, a whole bunch of stuff that he'll never in a million years have a chance to do one way or the other. It's how you keep from getting too down, I guess, when there aren't too many options.

So what did I do at the party? Not a hell of a lot. Mostly I had a few dumb conversations—one with a little huddle of guys who had a half-empty bottle of Jack Daniels they were passing around like a family heirloom and a few ridiculous theories on how you can tell a girl's a virgin by the sound of her voice or the way she laughs, and another with Shannon on what she believed were the hidden agonies of Quake's tortured soul. Usually I had one eye on who I was talking to and one on Diana. She wasn't with Condor every second, but they never seemed far away from each other, which is to say there was never a good opportunity of getting close to her without risking a fifteen-minute go-around with him. They were pretty touchy-kissy for two people not going out. Maybe they were married. When Diana sat on a couch and Condor decided to finish off one of his monologs with his head in her lap, I decided it was time to get some air.

I grabbed a fresh beer on my way out and popped it open once I was on the deck. The air didn't feel that cold at first, though I knew I'd feel it in my bones in less than a minute. All I had on was this old tweed sport jacket I like with skinny lapels and three buttons instead of two, which I never button—my signature garment, which Quake found in a secondhand store and gave me for my seventeenth birthday. I had the deck to myself except for a couple down at the other corner who seemed about to break up and retreated to a car when they saw me. I gave them an aluminum-can salute and took a long pull. I could have managed to take a leak about then, right off the deck, but I was in pretty clear sight. The stars were incredible, more than anybody could count, the way they get when the nights are supercold. A few barns and houses sparkled in the hills. A rush of light and music came from behind. I hoped the footsteps were Diana's.

It was Jennifer, though.

"Hey, Kyle, whatcha doing out here in the freezing cold?" she said, putting her hands on either side of my neck and leaning softly into me.

"Stargazing."

"You having a good time, sweetie?"

"Great time. Great party." I turned to face her. "Thanks for having me."

"Oh, Kylie, it wouldn't be a real party without you. God almighty!" she shrieked all of a sudden. "How can you stand it out here?"

"I'm a real Vamuntah. We like it a bit nippy."

She pulled my arm over her shoulder and pulled herself close to me. "You're warm," she said. "So what do you think about Diana and Condor?"

"Think about what?"

"They seem pretty hot for each other."

I had nothing to say about that.

"I think Diana's foolish," she said.

"She's the one's got to like him, not you."

"Oh, I love C.C.! I didn't mean that. He's a terrific guy. I just think she has choices that are better for her, that's all. Not that he isn't very sexy."

"Who'd you pick, then? Somebody unsexy?"

"I'd pick a real Vermonter."

"Those guys are a dime a dozen." I took another drink of beer. "Looks like one coming up the road right now."

8

ALL I'D MEANT WAS THAT THE FULL-SIZE PICKUP WITH the rusted-out muffler was just what a typical wood-chuck ought to be driving. The high beams and fog lamps blinded me totally as to who might be in the cab. But almost as soon as the driver put his boot on the ground, I knew who it was.

"Hey, David," I called out. "What you up to?"

"What *is* he up to? I didn't invite him," Jennifer said to me.

"Let me talk to him," I told her in a low voice.

I went quickly down the steps. Jennifer stayed on the deck.

"Is everything all right?" I said. "You need me for anything?"

"Nope. What I got to do I can do all by myself."

"And what would that be?"

"C.C. here?"

"He may be. What's up, dude?"

"He likes to start things with a big audience. I thought he might like the chance to finish one of them with an audience too."

"David Logan, you are not going to wreck my party!" Jennifer said. "You are not a guest here, so you can beat it." She'd have sounded more scary, except that she was shaking with cold by now.

"I ain't going nowhere near your party, Jenn."

"You're near it now."

"I'm staying right outside. You just let C.C. know I'm here. If he wants to come out, settle things like a man, fine. If he wants to hide in there with his girl-friends, I'll catch him later. You just tell him that."

"I'm not telling him anything. You leave or I'll call the cops."

She stormed across the deck to the front door. Of course even David had brains enough to know that the last thing Jennifer would do was call the cops. There were more underage drinkers in her house right now than you could fit into all the cruisers in Ira County.

"Dave, not here, huh," I said after she was gone.

"This don't concern you, Kyle—"

The rest of what he said was lost in the commotion that erupted behind me. I turned to see a bunch of kids pouring out onto the deck, with Condor right in front of them.

"Davy!" he called. "Man, am I glad to see you, bud."

Most of the faces behind him were grinning like a pack of hyenas. I had turned around so that I blocked the way off the last step.

"I've wanted to get in touch with you all weekend," Condor shouted, bounding down the stairs and just about pushing me out of the way.

"Yeah? And why's that?"

"I've seen a movie," Condor said.

Other guys were filing down the stairs now. I caught a glimpse of Diana on the deck just before I turned to face David again. Her face was asking me What?

"I saw this movie, David, and I swear, this movie"—Condor made a move that looked like he was slapping his hat on the ground—"this movie is the best darned, dang, gosh-darned movie you're ever, in your whole life, going to see."

David stepped closer to me for a moment. "Man can't hold his liquor," he said under his breath.

"Have you ever seen the movie *Deliverance*? Have you ever seen that movie?"

"No, I ain't," David said. He was opening and closing his fists, trying to stay loose.

"Well, you got to rent that movie tomorrow,

man. At the latest. It's an old movie, but it's a great movie, and you are going to love this movie. It's about these guys who go down the river and go hunting and fishing and do all these real man things that real rednecks like to do, and then they meet these other guys in the woods, and I swear to God, Davy, these other guys in the woods reminded me so much of you, I practically made a poopoo in my pants."

"You seen anybody that reminded you of yourself?"

"Yeah, sure," Condor said, bugging out his eyes. "The poor bastards that went down the river and met these other guys in the woods!"

The other kids laughed, including the girls on the deck. Some of them were running back inside for their coats. Condor did a quick run around David and then, with a move that was pretty awesome for a guy who supposedly couldn't hold his liquor, he sidevaulted over the tailgate and stood up in the truck bed.

"Hey, Davy," he called down. "What're these boxes in the back fer? This where you and the youngluns sleep?"

"Them's for my dogs, you fool," David said. "If you're that desperate for a bed, I'll let you borrow one."

Next Condor went into an Elvis routine, singing

"'You ain't nothin' but a hound dog,'" rolling his hips and bending down to shout into David's homemade kennels and then to David himself: "'They said you was high class. . . .'" The crowd liked this too, though some people had decided to go back inside. The next thing I knew, Diana was standing beside me. We exchanged one quick glance.

"Get the hell down from my truck!" David shouted, slamming his fist into the side of it. He went to throw a hold on the rails, but Condor stamped his foot on the edge several times.

"I tell you what, David. I'll get out of your truck if you get into it." Condor seemed wicked angry all of a sudden. "I don't belong in your truck—fine. You don't belong here. You get back in this garbage truck and I'll get out of it. How's that?"

You'd have thought Condor had just delivered the Gettysburg Address the way some people cheered and hooted. David was looking extremely frustrated just then, like he was cornered, and he seemed about to shove Diana aside when she stepped forward and took his arm.

"Why don't you drive me home," I heard her say. "Can you give me a ride?" She turned around and shouted, "Tell Jennifer I'm going. Is she still inside?" She was. "Tell her I said thanks."

"I can't drive you, Diana," David said. By now the

bystanders had gotten quiet enough for the nearest ones to hear what he said, though he talked in a pretty quiet voice. "The truck ain't all that clean, for one thing, and to tell you the truth, I've had a few myself. I wouldn't want to chance it."

"Ohhh," Condor sighed from the truck bed. "He's so sweet."

"Shut up," I said, not even bothering to look in his direction.

"Then you shouldn't drive yourself either," Diana said to David.

"Come with us," I said. "We're going to call Quake."

"I don't need to call no Quaker Oats. And I didn't mean to cause no trouble for you, Diana."

He gently moved us both aside.

"You best get out of there," he called to Condor. "This truck's laying down tracks."

He was in the cab before we could stop him. When Dave started the engine, Condor jumped out and lobbed a friend's bottle of beer at the truck as it pulled away. The glass shattered in the truck bed. Dave just kept driving. For now, at least, any spell Condor had over Diana was as broken as that bottle. When the time came to leave, there wasn't even a question that she was leaving with me.

•   •   •

Although he doesn't go to many parties, Quaker Oats is like the understood designated driver for the universe. All his friends and even some people who aren't his friends know that if they ever have too much to drink, no matter where they are or how late it is, they can call him up, and assuming he isn't already out giving another set of boozers a ride, he'll come to the rescue.

I know for a fact that his parents are not all that nuts about him driving around at all hours when every drunk driver is on the road too, but in the end this is their version of the compromise that all parents make who want to keep their kids safe without turning them into total dweebs. My mother's is to turn her head when she knows I'm drinking but to make it clear that if I ever drink and drive, or take a ride with someone who does, she'll torch my car and "use your license to start the fire." She means every word. The approach Quake's parents take is to let him answer a call like the one I put through to him after midnight.

I felt a little dumb that I had to. I'd drunk more than usual, assuming Diana would be going home with Condor and trying to get that whole thing off my mind. Now she was ready to go home with me, and I was too drunk to drive. But a ride with Captain Quake would be the next best thing, and he was most definitely, as he put it, on duty.

I was all set to take the front passenger seat, thinking the ladies might want to sit together, but at the moment of truth Diana gave me a little nudge toward the backseat. Then I realized the idea was to give Shannon the opportunity to moon over Quake, which suited me fine.

"You guys smell like a brewery," he said as he turned his old Datsun around to go out Jennifer's drive.

"We smell divine," Diana said. "We smell like God, right, Kyle?" She breathed on my face and said, "Worship me."

"I do," I said. I couldn't believe I'd said that. But all she did was lay her forehead on my shoulder and laugh.

"Hey, you guys, I think I finally figured out how we can make beer into a social protest project," Quake said. "This could wind up being really . . . bold."

"Is that what you guys are doing?" Shannon asked. "Beer?" She probably hadn't drunk much at the party. She never does.

"We're going to try," Quake said. "You could be a part of it too, if you wanted. Right, guys?"

"Sure," Diana and I said in unison.

"But what are you doing?" Shannon said.

"We don't know," I moaned.

"And we don't care," Diana said, laughing again.

"It was Kyle's idea to start with. Shannon, you were in class Friday, weren't you? Remember what Kyle said about Whalen's God question? It was brilliant, wasn't it?"

"Kyle does that a lot. He's always coming out with these really intelligent one-liners."

"No way," I said, though Quake and Diana disagreed. Shannon is like a lot of other girls I've known. She flirts with a guy she likes by saying all these great things about some other guy. I hoped Quake was suave enough to read the signals.

"Remember that time Mr. Whalen was trying to get us to say whether people were different now than way back in history or basically the same?" Shannon said. "And if you said we were different, you had to figure out what thing in history, like an invention or something, made us different?"

Diana began to rock her head like a metronome. "Before the written word, after the written word. Before the discovery of fire, after the discovery of fire. Before guns, after guns."

"You're drunk," I told her. "Woman can't hold her liquor."

"I only drank half a can," she whispered in my ear. "I'm just happy. Can't I be happy?"

"And Kyle said it was cars." Shannon was still going. "Remember?"

"I do!" Quake said. "I'd forgotten all about that. And it was the same thing as the beer answer, the car answer was. At first it seemed like—no offense, Kyle—a little on the simple side, but then when you thought about it, you realized that it was so totally perceptive. Cars did change everything. The way we work, the places we live—"

"The way we die, the places we screw."

"Kyle!" Shannon said. "I'm praising you and you're not behaving."

"It's all true, though . . ." Quake said, and on we drove, fogging the windows with a bunch of talk that sounded real deep then and wouldn't mean all that much in the morning. I had almost forgotten my car answer. If it wasn't for Quake I'd probably have forgotten the beer answer too. I remember him telling me, after class when I gave the car answer, that computers were changing the world even more than cars.

But I tell you what. Boot up your computer some morning and make it do everything it knows how to do. Print your baby pictures on a fifty-foot digital banner. Log onto the Net and chat with some champion pervert in Thailand. E-mail the pope. Design yourself a pair of cyber-kidneys and take a virtual leak. Run a CD-ROM with a graphic that builds the

Great Pyramids block by block and wraps all the mummies too.

Then when you're done all that, get into a car and, just to prove my point, make it a little tin piece of crap like Quake's. Get a few friends to go with you. If it's winter, crank up the heat; if it's summer, crank down the windows. Crank up the tunes no matter when it is and make them rock and roll, because as even Quaker Oats knows and will tell you straight out, it's the only music worth driving to. Watch that red needle climb to fifty, sixty, seventy-five on the straightaway and watch all the mountains, the barns, the silos, the trailers, the schools, the junkyards, the moose—everything except the big bright moon itself go sailing past.

Then you tell me what changes the world.

PART

1

FOR THE REST OF THAT NIGHT AND A GOOD PART OF
Sunday we put together our proposal for the Beer
Rebellion. Shannon had to go home, but Diana and I
were allowed to sleep over at Quake's house, which
we did. Shannon was able to come over Sunday afternoon—I picked her up after Quake drove me back to
Jenn's to get my car—and by suppertime we had our
proposal. Of course we'd taken a few good breaks
along the way, to eat, to listen to some of Quake's
weirder music, and to play a few games of Snakes out
on the ice.

On Monday Mr. Whalen agreed to meet with us
after school. Shannon couldn't come, and to tell you
the truth I think that she'd started to get cold feet
Sunday afternoon. Whalen started getting them as
soon as Quake said that we wanted to stage some "live
civil disobedience" as the main part of our project.

"In regard to what?" he said.

"Take it away, Kyle," Quake said. This took me by surprise for a moment, so I must have looked almost as spooked as Whalen did, because Quake was supposed to lay everything out with Diana and me acting as his assistants. But I realized what he meant for me to say when he repeated Whalen's original question: "According to Gandhi, God could only come to India as bread. How would God come to Willoughby Union?"

"Beer," I said.

Now Whalen was fully awake.

"And you want to do civil disobedience around beer?"

"Yes." Quake was all primed and ready to present, but Whalen jumped in first.

"If you're planning to violate liquor laws and do it as a school project, I think I'd prefer you to do it for somebody else's class. Am I on the right track here?"

"Partially," Quake said. "We plan to violate the liquor laws, true, but not just in the legal sense. We'd like to be a little more radical than that—"

"Maybe I should sit down."

"Yeah," Quake said. "That would be good."

Diana placed her hands on Whalen's shoulders and sat him down in one of the student desks. When I saw Quake take up a piece of chalk at the blackboard, I figured the best thing for me to do was erase the board, which I did. As my father would put it, I was "taking the backseat as per usual."

"Okay," Quake said. He drew a deep breath. Diana sat in the desk next to Whalen and folded her hands on top of it. I sat on top of another desk nearer the board.

What are the liquor laws? Quake wrote, and then underneath he wrote the word *Legal* with a dash and the number 21.

"You have to be twenty-one to drink," he said, "even though just about everybody drinks before they're twenty-one and everybody knows they do."

"I'm not sure I know that," Whalen said.

"Well, you know it now," I said. "Professor Oats has told you."

"Okay, but there are also social laws." Quake wrote *Social* next to *Legal* on the blackboard. "The social laws say that drinking is what makes you an adult."

"Drinking is what makes you social," Diana said.

"That too," Quake agreed. "So, *Drinking makes you an adult*"—he wrote the sentence as he said it—"and, like Diana said, *Drinking makes you social*. And the legal laws"—he pointed to where he'd written *Legal* on the board—"support this. Because they say you can vote, or join the army, or get married

75

when you're eighteen, you can drive even younger than that—"

"Or own a gun," Diana said.

"Not to mention becoming a parent at thirteen," Whalen said.

"Right, but it's like when you're a *real* adult you can finally do what's *really* important, what requires the *most* maturity and responsibility, which is drink a can of Budweiser. So in effect the legal law emphasizes the social law, and we intend to undermine both."

He threw the chalk down in the tray and dusted off his hands. First Diana and then I clapped. He stood there with this big shit-eating grin on his face, and you just had to love him. I looked over at Diana, and I could tell she was thinking the same thing.

"So where does your civil disobedience come in?" Whalen asked.

"Good question. But first I need to ask you a question."

"He sounds like you, Mr. Whalen," Diana said.

"I'd flunk him for being a wise guy," I said. "Impersonating a teacher."

"Here's the question." Quake held up one of his hands like a traffic cop. "What big advantage does civil disobedience have over violent resistance?"

"It's less violent," I said.

"It's more civil," Diana said.

"Now you see what I go through," Whalen said. "Make them figure it out, Quake. Don't tell them the answer."

"They already know the answer. We figured it out before we came."

"In that case, don't make me figure it out. Make it easy."

"Because . . . do you guys want to say it?" We shook our heads. "Because in a violent-type struggle all you see is how mad and how determined people are to fight against this thing they don't like. But with civil disobedience it's sometimes possible to give people a picture of what you'd prefer in place of what you're fighting against. It's like if you protest against a war peacefully, you can actually show people how peace is better than war. Does that make sense?"

"It makes perfect sense," Whalen said, "and it's all very insightful as usual. What I still don't see is how you intend to apply civil disobedience to the alcohol issue."

"We have three objectives: We want to lower the drinking age. We want to raise people's awareness of alcohol—medically, historically, culturally, every way we can. And third, we want to destroy the exaggerated status of drinking itself."

"Tell him about the parties," Diana said.

"We want to have parties, which are also like political demonstrations, and the idea is we have a group of high school students and some of them are drinking beer and the rest of the people aren't. But nobody knows what anybody else is drinking because the containers are all unmarked. You choose a container and you get what you get, either a beer or a soda. So it's no longer a big deal who's drinking or not because nobody even knows. So we're breaking a social law as well as a legal law. And if people have fun too, we've shown them a better way."

"And nobody overdoes it," I said.

"Or drives drunk," Quake continued, "and the way we handle that is with designated drivers. They're the only ones who we know whether they're drinking or not, and they're definitely not drinking."

"This is all great," Whalen said with a noisy sigh, "but what happens if our friends the police get wind of all this?"

It was one of those moments that Quake had been born for.

"Well, we have to *invite* them," he says, "otherwise they might not even have an opportunity to arrest us." Jeez'um, Whalen, get with it.

"As a school project, I have to be honest with you guys—"

"We'd do it all on our own time," Diana cut in. "Not to interrupt you, but we'd do it on our time—"

"Which you'd have to do anyway to have a real party," I said. "And never on school property."

"The only part of it that would be school-related," Quake said, "would be what we'd write up about it, like a journal or whatever you required, and we would each do our own, like giving our impressions, and we'd also do some research about the history of drinking and how different cultures handle it."

"Yeah, like in Spain there's no drinking age," I said. "If a little kid goes, 'I want my bottle,' you have to ask him which one."

"And Muslims don't drink at all," Diana said.

"Or Buddhists," Quake said.

"The thing is, guys, if you're doing something for me on this, something that you're getting credit for and I'm giving you a grade on, that makes me part of it, an accessory if you will. I'm just not sure I can go there. I don't want to cop out on you—I mean back in the Sixties . . ."

We tried a few different suggestions, but there was no way this would be a go. At first we were pretty bummed out about the whole thing, not that any of us wanted Mr. Whalen to lose his job because of us—we just wanted to do this and get credit for it if we could.

The day wasn't over, though, before all four of us—Shannon included—had made up our minds. We were going to do this thing, and screw the credit. In some ways it would be easier having school completely out of the picture. Quake said it would give our demonstrations "more legitimacy" in the eyes of the other students. Before the week was out, we'd all signed up for standard social studies reports. Shannon and Diana would team up and do the Women's Christian Temperance Union, which wanted to make alcohol illegal in America and for a short time got its way. Quake and I decided to research the Whiskey Rebellion, which took place shortly after the American Revolution when the government tried to force people to pay a tax to make their own whiskey, which they'd been doing for generations and which some people right here in Ira County can remember doing not that long ago. Our report on the Whiskey Rebellion was probably the reason we started calling our other thing the Beer Rebellion, though its official name was to be S.U.D.S.: Students Undermining a Drunk Society.

2

DAVID WASN'T IN SCHOOL THAT MONDAY. I DROPPED BY
the resource room a couple of times to check. It
wasn't unusual for him to miss a day of school—I bet
he never went five days straight in his life—but just
the same it was a relief to see him Tuesday morning
and to know that Saturday night's scene hadn't led
him to make good on his twice-a-month threat to dis-
appear into the deep woods of Maine or Canada
where there'd be "no math, no crap from anybody,
and no more scrounging for the old man."

When we passed in the hall between second and
third periods, he seemed in a really good mood, actually. I asked him if he was keeping out of trouble.

"Yup. And I'll tell you somebody else who's keeping out of trouble too."

I waited for the rest, pretty sure it would have to
do with Condor and almost completely sure there'd

been no incident since the party. I'd run into Condor a few times in the hall, and he didn't show any signs of damage.

"He passes by me now and he don't say nothing. He don't even want to look at me."

"Well, good. Just leave it at that then. He knows now you won't take any crap. Don't look at him either. It's done."

"That's how I work. If a man leaves me alone, I leave him alone."

I told him that was a good idea and said I'd catch him later. Now if I could just be sure that Condor would leave Diana alone too. But I had seen them yesterday afternoon at her locker, with him looking so truly sorry and well behaved it was pathetic, and her wearing that expression a girl gets that can only mean one of two things: She's either won a million in the lottery or just discovered a new psychopath she believes she can reform.

I stopped in the resource room after social studies, thinking I might eat my lunch there like I had last Friday. I didn't do it that often, and I wasn't planning on making it a regular thing either. I just felt I ought to go there today now that David was back in school. I suspect that deep down I felt a little guilty about not giving David more backup Saturday night. Until

Diana got involved, I was pretty much standing in the neutral zone. True, he'd come to Jennifer's looking for trouble, but I know if our situations had been reversed, he would have been right there for me.

Only a couple of kids were in the room besides Dave. He was over in his usual corner by the window with his massive back to the door and a pair of headphones on. He was sort of rocking to the beat of whatever was playing, and it struck me funny to see him nodding his big bushy head like that, as if he really was Davy Crockett and had just taken a break from choking a panther to check out AM 1809, "the Tennessee mountains' *big* rock station." I knew if I went up to him and he called me "dude" with those headphones on, it just might be more than I could handle with a straight face. Mrs. Cantor was eating her squirrelly lunch at her desk. I decided to hang with her until David noticed I was there.

"Mind if I have a little lunch with you?"

"No, not at all. You can have your lunch here every day if you want."

I held up my donation before dropping it in the can and snagging a soda from her fridge.

"So what are you studying these days, Kyle?"

"Beer."

It was so funny, because I popped open my can of soda just as I said "beer" and Mrs. Cantor did this double take like she expected me to have miraculously found a Silver Bullet in her little refrigerator.

"Beer? What are you studying that in? Health class?"

"Social studies. We're doing like this . . . I guess you could call it a demonstration, and we're getting some interesting background stuff to go with it. Did you know the ancient Egyptians were one of the first people to brew beer?"

"No, but it doesn't surprise me. They were an amazing civilization."

"Yup. They found this picture in a tomb or a pyramid or whatever, and it shows this slave, and underneath it says, 'My master gives me bread and beer and every good thing.'"

I could tell she had something to say but wanted to swallow her mouthful of nuts and raisins first.

"Of course it's not a slave saying that, is it? It's the master," she said.

"What do you mean?"

"Well, it's not the slave who wrote that inscription. The slave probably didn't even know how to write. It was the master speaking *for* the slave. Masters like to think their slaves are happy."

"Well, look at it this way. If the master gave them beer, maybe they *were* happy."

"Maybe that's why he gave it to them."

"Uh-huh." It seemed that I was missing something all of a sudden, though I wasn't sure what.

"Along the same lines, did you know that they repealed Prohibition during the Great Depression because with so many people destitute, all the well-to-do people were afraid of a revolution? They gave the unemployed people beer to make them happy too."

"No, I didn't know that," I said. I glanced over at Dave, who was still into his music. He was working on something too, but all the time rocking to the beat.

"Okay, here's another one," I said. "Did you know that if the ancient Persians had a very important decision to make, they'd think about it sober and then they'd get drunk and think about it again?"

"Really? No, I didn't." She chewed very slowly for a second. "Is Quaker Oats involved in this little project of yours, by any chance?"

There was just the slightest sparkle in her eye that said she was taking everything from here on in with a grain of salt. I said he was, and was all set to swear to God about the Persians when she matched me fact for fact once again.

"And the ancient Greeks knew about fetal alcohol syndrome. I only know that because I took a course in F.A.S. last fall. Apparently they wouldn't let a new bride drink wine. . . ."

I was amazed to see her blushing.

"Okay, last fact," I said. "Did you know that you can buy a six-pack of Molson Ice for five ninety-nine at the Salmon Falls Mini-Mart all this week?"

"No," she said, folding up her lunch garbage and trying not to smile. "I'm not really a beer drinker. And I hope you're not either, Kyle."

"Oh, I don't know, Mrs. Cantor. You strike me as the type who likes to party hearty on the weekend."

"Mostly, Kyle, I like to recover on the weekend. The hearty stuff is Monday through Friday for me. Like with your pal over there." She stood up, smiling in his direction, and patted my shoulder. "Why don't you say hi to Dave before you go. He's always glad to see you."

He didn't seem glad to see me when I came over, though. Maybe I just startled him, I thought. He couldn't hear me coming with his headphones on.

"Hey, dude, what you listening to?"

I went to grab his headphones, which guys do with each other all the time—so I was shocked for a couple of seconds when he pushed my hand away with this extremely ugly expression on his face. His hand must have accidentally caught the headphone wire and disconnected it from the unit.

It was one of those half minutes that seem to last for an hour. Dave jumped up and stared at me with his face all twisted up and the useless headphones still clamped to his ears. Did he wonder for just an instant where the music had gone to? It was blasting from the speaker of the tape recorder, this Dracula-voiced guy rapping out the multiplication tables with howling wolves and ghoulish cackles in the background: "Three times vive is vifteen, vour times vive is twenty, vive times vive is twenty-vive—you are so smart, darling, it scaaares me!"

"David, you want to turn that down a bit," Mrs. Cantor called from the other side of the room. She was bent over another kid's desk, totally unaware of what was happening.

I gave David a faint little smile, which I'm sure he took for me making fun of him. The words were barely out of Mrs. Cantor's mouth before he tore the headphones off and smashed the tape recorder onto the floor. What the fall didn't demolish one of his steel-toed work boots did.

"David, what on earth's the matter?" Mrs. Cantor cried. He was moving to the door and stopped right in front of her before storming out of the room.

"I ain't coming in here ever again, I swear!" he shouted into her face.

By the time I passed her on my way after David,

she was pretty shaken up. She was all set to blame me too.

"What did you say to him?" she said.

"I didn't say nothing," I shouted.

So in the space of a minute two guys had yelled in her face.

As things turned out, this wouldn't be the last time, but as far as I can remember it was the first time I ever cried in high school. I knew better than to follow David, who was clear down to the other end of the hall when I saw him, so I took the stairs down and practically threw myself into the exit doors. I stood outside in the dirty snow and just started bawling. I couldn't help it. On the stairs I'd met Jennifer Burch, probably the last person on earth I wanted to see or have see me then, and she'd called after me, "Kyle, are you all right?"

Of course she had to come find me, even though I'd ducked around the corner of the building. I was pretty far gone by then.

"What's wrong, Kyle?" she said, all set to crawl all over me. "Is it something to do with Diana?"

That really ticked me off—so much that for a moment I could stop crying. "It doesn't have to do with Diana!" I yelled. I swore besides. So I felt I had to say "please" when I told her to leave me alone.

"You can always talk to me, Kyle," she called out on her way into the building. "You can tell me anything, hon."

But what was there to tell her? I wasn't even sure why I was crying. It wasn't that I felt guilty—I hadn't done anything wrong, and Cantor could take a flying you-know-what for all I cared just then. David was always getting pissed about one thing or another—I was practically used to that. It was just that it hit me all of a sudden, like a twelve-gauge shotgun going off in my guts, how totally stupid our little world was. All day long I kept seeing the shame on David's face when his earphones came loose. All day long I kept thinking about those Egyptian slaves with their bread and their beer and their heads up their party-hearty rear ends.

3

THE NEXT DAY WAS WEDNESDAY, WHICH MEANT WE WERE only a week and a half away from our first "action," as Quake called it. We had written up the rules: no drugs, no beverages but what we supplied, no beverages in original containers, no alcohol besides beer, no drunks. Shannon said we shouldn't make our party open or even known to anybody else besides ourselves and our invited guests. She was pretty persuasive. She argued that even regular parties are just for certain people, but Quake said that any restrictions would defeat our whole purpose.

"People are excluded from social acceptance if they don't drink—so how can we make that one of the things we're protesting and then have a private party? It has to be open. It just has to be."

"I think you're asking for trouble," Shannon said, but in the end Diana and I voted with Quake. As a compromise we agreed not to make any public announcement of the project until the same Friday as the action—the same day we would fax or e-mail *The Salmon Falls Republican* with our "statement," which was pretty much a repeat of the things we'd told Whalen, including our objectives: to lower the drinking age, inform people about drinking, and make drinking itself less of a big deal in the local social scene. We wouldn't call the cops until the party was under way; otherwise, they might try to stop our civil disobedience before it even started.

Of course there was one other piece in the notification category, and that had to do with telling our parents what was up. We all felt we'd get in less trouble if our parents were spared the shock of finding out about everything afterward. On the other hand, if we told them ahead of time, they might try to stop us or at least make things more difficult. My parents and Diana's knew we drank, or at least hers seemed to know. My mom definitely knew. Shannon's parents didn't know at all, but then she drank so little it almost didn't seem to matter, although she said it would matter a lot. And Quake, of course, didn't drink at all, so it would seem very strange to his parents, not to mention that he was basically the brains behind the whole thing. (He did say that if he drew a beer at the party, he'd drink it, which we all thought would be kind of cool.)

In the end Diana convinced us not to tell and to just take our chances. We knew if we told our parents, they'd be upset, even parents like my mom, because this was more than just a couple of beers on the sly, whereas it could happen that we'd be more or less ignored and nobody'd have to get upset at all.

"Until the next action," Quake said.

Eighth period Quake and Diana had off, and I was able to get out of English by promising to make up the film we were watching on my own time, so we could do some work together down in the cafeteria and talk more on the unsolved problems, like where we were actually going to do this thing. Obviously we couldn't do it at any of our houses if we weren't telling our parents, and there weren't that many kids we could ask either, if we wanted to keep the lid on things till next week.

"Did you ever get to ask Reggie Barton about using his place?" Quake said.

"He don't want any part of it. He wouldn't even let me finish explaining it."

"This is so funny," Diana said. "The Bartons have big parties all the time where everybody is drinking. The cops have been up there at least twice."

"They're mainly just trying to keep Reggie off the road, though," I said. "His parents, I mean."

"I know, but when you compare what they let him and his friends do and what we want to do, which is a hundred times more tame—"

"In a way," Quake said. "In another way not. We're cutting through the hypocrisy, which is the opposite of tame."

"How's your list?" I asked Diana. I didn't feel like having Quake get off on one of his tangents. At Shannon's suggestion, we were "decorating" our party with various pieces of information. Right then Diana was putting some of them on a poster.

"Pretty good," Diana said. "For famous drinkers I've got Alexander the Great—"

"Major lush," Quake said.

"—Jesus Christ—"

"Jesus Christ?" Quake and I said at the same time. A couple of the kids in the cafeteria looked up. They must have thought we were swearing.

"Yeah, not like a big boozehound or anything, but . . . who's got the quote sheet? There's something from the Bible that Shannon found."

Quake had a copy of the quote sheet in the small suitcase he uses in place of a backpack.

"She found millions of quotes," he said.

"Wants to impress you, Quake," I said.

"All right here it is," he said. I think I'd embarrassed him. "'For John the Baptist has come eating no bread and drinking no wine, and you say, "He has a demon"; the Son of Man has come eating and drinking, and you say, "Look, a glutton and a drunkard, a friend of tax collectors and sinners!" Nevertheless, wisdom is vindicated by all her children.'"

"So you could put John the Baptist with the famous nondrinkers," I said.

"I already did," Diana said. "Other famous drinkers: Dylan Thomas, Bonnie Prince Charlie, Lord Byron, Janis Joplin, James Agee, Socrates—who they say could drink all he wanted and never get drunk—Ulysses S. Grant, Winston Churchill. Famous nondrinkers: Carry Nation, Buddha, Adolf Hitler, Mohammed, Samuel Johnson, Friedrich Nietzsche, Malcolm X, Tecumseh—"

"The nondrinkers have the weirder names," I said. "*Tecumseh.*"

"He was a Native American chief. According to Shannon, Tecumseh's whole tribe was in danger of becoming alcoholic," Diana said. "Liquor was one of the weapons the whites were using against them. It was really his brother who was the big nondrinker. He was like a prophet or something, and he tried to get his people to stop drinking, but no one's heard of him. That seemed even more obscure."

"Not-so-famous nondrinkers of history: Tecumseh's brother," Quake said.

"Quake's aunt Sadie," I said.

"I actually have an aunt Sadie! I'm serious."

"I met her, remember? All right, you people," I said. "Listen up. Here's mine. My motto." I was looking at Shannon's list of quotes. "John Steinbeck, *The Grapes of Wrath*: 'Like to stay drunk all the time. Who says it's bad? Who dares to say it's bad? Preachers—but they got their own kinda drunkenness. Thin, barren women, but they're too miserable to know. Reformers—but they don't bite deep enough into living to know. No—the stars are close and dear and I have joined the brotherhood of the worlds. And everything's holy—everything, even me.'"

I didn't say it to Quake and Diana, but I'd actually felt that way once or twice myself when I was loaded. I wondered if my father felt that way when he was loaded. I wondered if anybody ever felt that way when they were not.

When I saw Mrs. Cantor heading toward us with that little missionary determination in her step, I got up from the table. I had told Quake and Diana that David was pissed off at me, but I hadn't gone into all the details.

"You want to talk to me, right?"

"No, Kyle, not just you. May I sit down?"

She sat on the other side of the table, next to Diana.

"I'd like to talk to all of you if you have a minute. I need some help. Or David does."

"I'm really sorry," I offered, sitting down again.

She reached across the table and took my hand, which startled me.

"You have nothing to be sorry about, Kyle. It was all my fault."

"How's it your fault, though?"

"It's my fault for not providing David with age-appropriate materials."

She looked so upset that Diana actually started to rub her back. She stopped when it seemed to be making things worse.

"It's just not easy to find things . . . for people your age, and David seemed to be amused by the tape—I hadn't even gotten that one for him; it came with something else I ordered, but he latched onto it and was making progress with it, and . . . I should have been more sensitive. He was bound to be embarrassed and that's exactly what happened. Through no fault of yours, Kyle."

"Hey," Quake chimed in, "age is all relative. For most stuff it's meaningless."

"Not when you're out of your teens and still in

high school," she said. "The world has these arbitrary ideas about what everybody ought to be doing by a certain age, and it can be awfully unforgiving of those who don't fit the mold."

Looking right then at Mrs. Cantor, who'd pulled a tissue out of the cuff of her sweater and was wiping her nose, I wanted so badly to say, "The world can eat it." Instead I said, "You were saying we could help."

"Yes. But I'm not sure you can, Kyle. Not yet at least. I think you and I are still on David's blacklist. He'll come around eventually, I'm sure. The thing is, David is this close"—she brought two of her fingers half an inch shy of together—"to passing his math from last semester, which is still incomplete, but I fear he won't make it without some help. And now he won't so much as talk to me. He bombed his first quarter pretty badly, mostly on account of poor attendance, but Mrs. Solinsky says if he passes this marking period she'll pass him for the course even if he blows off the midyear. I thought if there was someone I could coach behind the scenes who'd be willing to coach David . . ."

"Sure," Quake said.

"He might not deal with you because we're friends," I said.

"You think he'd work with me?" Diana asked. "We're all friends, as far as that goes, but maybe because I'm not a guy he wouldn't see it as much?"

Mrs. Cantor turned to face her, which meant she had to look up.

"I bet he might work with you, dear. It wouldn't take a great deal of your time."

"Don't worry about it."

"You know David doesn't have many opportunities to spend time with a pretty girl."

Diana looked uncomfortable for a second, but then she tossed back her hair and said, "Neither do these guys. That's why I try to keep them company now and then."

"I see—"

"Yeah, Mrs. Cantor," Quake said, "maybe you could keep us company while Diana's busy helping David, you know, so we don't lose the feminine perspective."

That got her going. "Oh dear, well, you know you're always welcome in my room, but I'm sure you fellows can find better female company than some old bag."

"Really, they can't," Diana said. I made as though I might smack her.

"You know, seriously though, your being as tall as you are . . . David always feels so self-conscious that because of his size, everyone will know he's a little older. With you, I think he'll feel more comfortable."

"I hope so."

Now it was Diana's hand that she touched.

"And you may find you have to remind him to settle down to business. David can be quite the little socializer, you know."

I couldn't get over her calling David "the little socializer," when as near as I could tell he had the social life of a rock. But like Mrs. Cantor had said, the world has these ideas.

Diana began working with David that Friday, exactly one week from the start of the Beer Rebellion.

4

WE DECIDED TO HOLD OUR PROTEST PARTY AT STEVIE'S,
which is an enormous abandoned barn that overlooks
a stretch of the southbound interstate. It's called
Stevie's because the name appears in three-foot-high
red letters along with a whole bunch of graffiti that
was painted in honor of Steven Bouchard after he
drove his car into the rear of a parked tractor trailer
at eighty-five miles an hour and decapitated himself.
This happened on the night of his graduation, at the
end of my freshman year. There was some talk a
while back of painting the barn over, but come to
find out it was the property of a distant Canadian relative of his who only used the barn to store old farm
machinery in anyway and who wanted to keep the
memorial. So Stevie's name and the giant pictures
of his face (or, as some like to say, his head), his
Trans Am, his foamy beer mug, and his classmates'

yearbook-style good-byes have stayed right where they are, though each year the paint grows fainter than the year before, and there are now kids at school who don't even know who Steven Bouchard was.

Quake felt the location was symbolic, not only because of Stevie and his death in an alcohol-related accident, but because kids do park there and drink once in a while, though usually in the warmer weather. We were going in late February.

Quake and I arrived first, then Shannon and Diana. To celebrate her most successful season ever, Diana's parents had put together a couple of milk checks and bought her a not-so-used red Subaru with a roof rack and four-wheel drive. She wouldn't be needing too many lifts from me now. We parked along the fire lane that passes Stevie's on the back side. The drive to the barn had not been plowed since the last snowstorm, so we had to haul everything around to where we'd be setting up the party in an empty tractor shed. The barn itself was padlocked.

Lucky for us the weather was not too cold. We were in the middle of a major thaw, which we usually got in January and which was not usually this warm. We'd get clobbered again in March, of course, but for now everybody was pretending to wonder if spring had actually come early. The snow was slushy under our feet; a border of bare ground surrounded the barn.

We ran along it, chasing each other like little kids, once we'd set up. First we had mounted Shannon's boom box on a cross beam inside the shed. Rule number one: Get some music going before you do anything else. We set out a couple of card tables with food and "anonymous" drinks. We built a pretty good campfire outside the shed using dry wood we'd brought from Quake's house. We fired up Quake's portable generator, setting it as far from the shed as we could to lessen the noise, and strung wires for a few party lights. We set the blue plastic tub with the word TUB written on it as close to the campfire as we dared. The idea was that if the cops came, we would all toss our containers into the tub. The cops would have to decide then whether to test us all or bust us all or just tell us all to go home.

Last of all we hung up our information posters and charts, including a large bedsheet with our "demands":

LOWER THE DRINKING AGE
RAISE THE DRINKER'S AWARENESS
DESTROY THE NONDRINKER'S STIGMA

Then, like I said, we ran around the barn for a while.

We stopped at one point to catch our breath, standing under the Stevie mural and looking out at the cars and logging trucks barreling along I-91. Not that there were many here at the edge of the world. It was dark by then, and we could just make out the ghostly surface of Salmon Pond with its black mound of island, one of my favorite sights in the whole world. We had two flashlights—for a minute we spaced them like headlights and shone them at the highway for no good reason except that we felt like it. Then we turned and gave Stevie's peeling face the spotlight. Shannon said, "Hi there, Stevie."

"You know, I just thought of something," Quake said. "We should've put Stevie on our famous-people list. He's sort of famous around here."

"On which side would you put him, though?" I said. "Drinker or nondrinker?"

"Both. That's why I wish we'd thought of it."

Quake, Diana, and I had talked a lot about Stevie's death after it happened, but Shannon was apparently in the dark about Stevie's history. So Quake filled her in. Stevie had been a big drinker in high school, one of those guys who drink so much and at such crazy times of the day that even big drinkers start to say he's got a problem, though that's mainly to point out that they themselves don't have a problem. It was no wonder Stevie was like he was, his old man being notorious as a lush himself. All of a sudden, sometime in his senior year, Stevie swore off drinking. Some people said it was a girlfriend, other people said he'd had a close call on the road one night, and I'd also heard the story that he gave it up after his old man got stinking one day and beat the crap out of his mother to the point that Stevie decided that the life just wasn't for him. No one really was sure. The thing is, at least as I heard it, a lot of his old friends stopped hanging around with him so much. He was still welcome at the parties he'd gone to before, but there was less point in going now. It just wasn't the same. He got bored; he went back to drinking. You know the rest.

So Quake was right. Stevie Bouchard had something in common with the famous drinkers and the famous nondrinkers too. He would have no matter what because, like most of the people on either list, he was dead.

By nine or so we had about nine or ten of the twenty people we'd specially invited and several others who came by way of the general announcement. After we thanked people for coming, we had them choose a container from the beverage table. Most of the containers were filled with soda, but three had beer—the four of us organizers had shuffled them around before the party began, so that even we didn't know which was which. If somebody came in and said they definitely wanted soda, we would take one out of the cooler and disguise it for them. We didn't want anybody to be forced to drink a beer if they didn't want to.

Everything was pretty well organized, I'd say, but that didn't stop some people from being first-class pains from the get-go. One guy had to blurt out that he'd gotten "lucky" after he took his first sip. So much for his drink being a secret. Then a couple people complained that they wanted a different flavor soda from the one they drew off the table. I was starting to understand why Gandhi had done his protest with fasting—that way you can weed out the jerks. Make it fun enough for everybody to get involved, and pretty soon you won't be having fun.

But after a while things did warm up, I have to admit, both party-wise and protest-wise too. You could feel a little buzz in the crowd, a nervous kind of expectation based on knowing that we were doing something we'd always done but in a brand-new way. Of course everybody wanted to know when we were "going to do it," that is, call the cops. A few people even read the posters. A couple of people bitched about the dampness and the cold, but we did have the fire, and after a while we'd packed down enough snow to dance. Also, I'd had the good luck, or the bad, to draw a beer.

I noticed a little huddle around Quake about the

same time as a lot of other people did, and in another moment we were all crowded around this older guy from *The Republican* who'd been sent over to cover our story. He looked something like a small-time pot dealer, which is to say like almost every newspaper reporter I've ever seen.

Quake was saying how the idea began in social studies class, which led the reporter to ask, "So there are teachers behind this then?"

"No," about three of us said at once. Quake called for somebody to turn down the music. I got a whiff of his breath. He definitely hadn't drawn a beer.

"But this began in school basically."

"We go to school," I said. "That's where we see each other. Everything begins in school."

"And what is it you hope to prove?"

"We're not trying to prove anything," Diana said.

The reporter looked up at her and said, "I'm surprised to find you at something like this, LaValley. Shouldn't you be home answering mail from all those eager Division One college recruiters?"

The guy's attitude was getting to me, but before I had a chance to tell him so, I saw him jerk forward like he was about to do some serious projectile vomiting. And who should be right behind him saying a real smart-ass "Excuse me" but Condor Christy.

•　•　•

The reporter stuck around. After swearing a bit, he went off to do some further muttering in a corner. Diana and Shannon walked over to offer him some food. Quake had some words with Condor about the nature of civil disobedience. I stayed nearby in case Condor tried to get smart with him. In his usual sarcastic way he promised to be on his best behavior. He had just been accepted into this "top-of-the-line" art school, he said, so he was going to clean up his act. Also, he made a point of telling me that he'd promised my "sister" to be good. Of course Quake had to offer his congratulations and ask the name of the school. I didn't stay to hear it.

Quake tapped my shoulder a few minutes later—I was about to dance with Shannon—and I turned around to see him with his mother's cell phone. It was time. He no sooner pulled up the antenna than it seemed to call in the kids by magic; they were all around us, with the firelight shining in some faces and shadowing others. The reporter came too. Quake and I were eyeball-to-eyeball. I looked for Diana, but she wasn't there. Neither was Condor.

"You want to do it?" Quake asked.

It was one of those times when you have to know a friend really well, because at that moment you can believe either of two things about him, one being very good and the other pretty bad. From what I heard later, some people were ready to believe the bad thing, namely that Quake had lost his nerve at the last minute. Maybe I wondered the same thing, but only the tiniest shameful bit. What I knew for sure was that Quake is the kind of guy who doesn't need to be the hero all the time, though sometimes he simply can't help it. The job just seems to catch up with him.

I was less sure about myself. I handed the phone back to Quake. I'd like to know even now if I was chickening out or just trying to be as generous as he was. Anyway, he started to dial, and everybody told everybody else to shut up. After giving his name and our location, he read this message from a piece of paper he had folded in his pocket.

"My friends and I, all of whom are under the age of twenty-one, are drinking illegally tonight in civil disobedience against laws that we consider unjust and social customs that we consider equally unjust. We are not asking to be arrested, but we wish to give you that option."

Apparently nobody was saying anything on the other end.

"Are you there?" Quake said. "Oh . . . well, that's all I had to say. Have a nice evening. Good-bye."

Everybody cheered—everybody that is, except Diana and Condor, who were still AWOL. And then, almost immediately, we heard the roar of half a dozen snowmobiles heading in our direction. Their headlights strafed the barnyard. We looked at each other, all wondering the same thing: Did the cops know about our party all along? How could they get here so fast?

The drivers killed their engines all at once. About half a dozen guys from school, including a couple who'd been out for a year or two, got off their machines and swaggered over with a couple of cases of beer and a generally hostile attitude. Reggie Barton was one of them, and I usually get along pretty good with Reg, but he had already had a few and had that dazed and potentially nasty gleam in the eyes.

"You're on our spot," he said to me.

One of the other riders was already at the beverage table. I saw him take one of the containers, sip, and spit a stream of soda on the ground.

"What's this shit?" he demanded.

"Friends, friends . . ." Quake took Reggie by the arm, but Reggie knocked his hand away. "The police are coming. If you read our circulars at school—"

"I didn't read your circulars at school. I might have accidentally wiped my ass with one, though. How do you know the cops are coming?"

"I called them up to invite them," Quake said.

I was right next to Quake. "It's true, Reg," I added.

By this time our friends must have told Reggie's friends the same thing, because one of them was calling to him, and a few others were rushing over to where we stood. But Reggie just kept staring at Quake.

"You did what? Are you trying to bullshit me?"

Before either Quake or I could say no, Shannon shrieked that the police were here. Sure enough, their blue strobes were pulsing along the access road, and in less than a minute we heard a megaphone squawk.

"Tub!" Quake shouted, which was our signal to toss. Had it been just us, the total alcohol content of the tub would have been the equivalent of two or three beers, no more. As it was, cans and bottles got dropped and flung every which way as the party crashers made tracks for their snowmobiles. Quake kept calling, "Tub!" What a laugh! The place looked like a saloon after a world-class rumble.

There were only two cops, and they ordered us to stand where we were. When I looked around I only counted five people, including myself. Diana and Condor were not part of the five. Poor Shannon, who had never in her life gotten so much as an after-school detention, had tears running down her cheeks. She didn't try to run, though.

Quake was giving his little speech welcoming the officers and promising our full cooperation, which I have to say he delivered fairly calmly for someone standing in a junkyard of leaking beer cans with a high-powered flashlight glaring in his face. One of the cops yelled, "Hold it right there," and I turned to see Diana and Condor jog to an abrupt stop at the edge of the campfire light. They must have come back from wherever they'd wandered off to, when they heard the commotion. Diana was still holding her container.

"I'm going to ask you to pass what's in your hand to me, miss," the cop said, stepping toward her. I remember hearing nothing but wood crackling in the fire.

Diana raised her arm, and I would have bet my life's savings, if I hadn't already blown them on a car, that Diana could have gotten that container into the tub with her eyes closed.

But she hadn't taken more than a step forward when Condor grabbed the container out of her hand and, as Quake groaned in disgust, tried to make a run for it. The other cop grabbed hold of him, and then the one in front of Diana turned to help, because Condor was thrashing around like a wild animal. He would not let go of Diana's container.

It was the reporter, of all people, who eventually got it away from him. "I'll take a look at that, young man." I thought for a second the cops were going to drop Condor and muckle onto that guy. But before they could even ask what the heck he was doing, he'd torn the cap off the container—I guess he wasn't going to drink through anybody else's straw if he could help it—and taken a swallow.

The look on his face . . . and on Condor's face too.

"For God's sake, it's nothing but a soda."

5

EXCEPT FOR PUTTING CONDOR IN HIS PLACE, THE COPS were actually pretty friendly to us that night. One of them said, "This was a first, I'll tell you," and he seemed to get a kick out of that. Our parents were a different story.

"I thought we talked to each other, you and me," my mother said when I fessed up the next morning.

"We're talking now, aren't we?"

"It's a little late, Kyle."

"I just didn't want you to worry when there might not be anything to worry about."

"Quaker Oats—or should I say Quaker Nuts— calls the cops to come to a drinking party and you thought there might be nothing to worry about?"

"They might have taken it as a joke." Weak, but possible.

"It's not a joke. And anyway, you weren't worried

about me worrying. You were worrying about me trying to interfere with your little escapade. That's the truth of it."

"None of us told our parents, Mom."

"Mm-hm. And none of us, it turns out, was drinking when the cops got there except good old Kyle."

"I told you how we worked it out. And anyway, other people were drinking—"

"Not Diana, not Shannon, and definitely not Quake. Let me finish. Do you find anything strange, because I sure do, that all your preppy friends managed to wind up with a soda but my son, Kyle, the towny boy whose parents work in the mill—"

"This is not fair."

"My point, Kyle. You hit the nail right on the head. Not fair. When it comes to who's got all the advantages, it never is. Honey, look at me."

I could handle her except when she got like this, with her eyes suddenly not mad anymore and her hand on top of mine. The extra-hoarse voice didn't help either. She'd have to step out for a smoke when she was done talking, all on account of me.

"I know what it's like for people your age. You guys think of friendship like it's a religion. A.F.F., right? A Friend Forever. They were writing that in yearbooks back when I went to school. Let's keep in touch, and if you ever need a kidney transplant . . . It's like a lot of other things people pretend to believe in—what they really believe in is taking care of themselves. And they will, every time. You can bank on it. You got to be your own friend too, Kyle."

"Can we finish this?"

"We can, yes. But your father wants to see you."

"What for?"

"How long have you lived around here, Kyle? Your father called me and told me about everything before you were even out of bed this morning. There are no secrets in a town like this. . . . Hey! We don't use that word in this house."

Going to see my father after school on Monday was most of what I thought about that day, and although I was anything but looking forward to it, I have to say it came in handy as something to take my mind off everything else. I hadn't felt so bummed out in a long time—or I guess since David unhooked his tape recorder. He wasn't in school much these days, or else he was doing a good job of avoiding me if he was.

The guys who'd crashed the party were walking around like it was a big joke, and there were plenty of people who seemed to share their opinion. Everything about us was "stupid." It was stupid to have a party outdoors in February. It was stupid to let the cops know we were drinking. It was even stupid to want to lower the drinking age. Oh yeah. You wouldn't believe the number of big-time drinkers who said so. A few people were sympathetic, I guess. I didn't want to hear anything from anybody. I especially didn't want to hear another version of how the mighty Condor had dove to Diana's rescue and wrestled with two cops and a reporter or how he and Diana had been seen together at a pizza place in Angle Junction the next night.

"Why did Diana make such a big deal out of trying to throw her container into the tub if she was only drinking soda anyway?" I asked Quake at his locker.

"That was the game plan. You know Diana. She always plays with the team."

"She didn't seem to be playing with the team too much from what I could see. Where the hell was she, anyway?"

"Same deal," Quake said. "One-on-one defense. She was trying to keep Condor from screwing things up for the rest of us."

"The only thing he wants to screw—"

Reggie Barton was in our faces before I could finish.

"You call the cops on me, Quaker Oats?"

"He called the cops before you showed up, Reg,

and you know it," I said. Boy, I was not in the mood for him.

"I hope I never find out any different."

"What are you going to do then, Reggie, fight him? Go toe-to-toe with a pacifist? That'd take real guts, wouldn't it?"

Reggie smiled and gave my shoulder a little shove. "You ain't a pacifist, though, are you?"

I shoved him back, no harder than he'd shoved me. "Let me know whenever you want to find out," I said. He laughed and got back into the traffic. We both knew he could whip my ass any day.

About the only good thing that happened that whole lousy Monday was when Jennifer Burch, who hadn't come to our party and would never be caught dead at something so stupid, stopped at my locker and gave me a wet kiss on the cheek.

She might have been saying good-bye, and the way she shook her head afterward seemed to say as much. But when I thought to myself "What the heck" and hugged her close to me, she definitely did not pull away.

My father's theory has always been that I do everything for spite, mostly to spite him, even though I hardly ever try to spite anybody and never give him so much as a thought.

"This is all spite, Kyle."

What else was new?

We were at the plant, standing in front of his machine, an injection blow-mold setup the size of a propane truck. The two sides of the mold press together like a giant hydraulic vise, the hot plastic shoots in, the mold opens with a loud hiss, and a set of four hot empty jugs drops on the conveyor belt. My dad pulls the jugs off the little plastic tree and trims the waste from their seams with a sharp curved knife. Then another set drops just like before. He was on break now. That's when I sometimes go over, mostly to keep the visits short. The machine was idling at our backs. High above us, along the upper edge of the far wall, a bit of pale sunshine came through a row of frosted windows and got lost in the fluorescent light banks below.

"Spite toward you, I suppose."

"What else would you call somebody with your background drinking all the time?"

My father's built like me, medium but rugged, except he's got a small beer gut. He had his arms crossed over his dark-blue T-shirt, a pack of smokes in his front pocket, bags under his eyes. He hadn't shaved that morning. I couldn't help wondering if this was what I'd look like at forty-one.

"What do you mean my 'background'?" I said.

"I know your mother turns a blind eye because she thinks there's nothing she can do—you'll only drink anyway. But now you're putting it in her face, she sees what's come of that approach. If I were in the house, we'd have a different arrangement, I'll tell you that much."

"Well, you're not in the house, are you?" Another advantage to meeting my father at work is that there's usually somebody walking by, even on breaks, so I can mouth off without worrying he's going to smack me.

"And why ain't I in the house, smart guy?"

"I've always wanted to know that, actually."

"I ain't in the house, living with my family, because when I was your age, and a bit older, I did everything you do. I was a spiteful little son of a bitch too. I drank too much and I didn't try to better myself. Sound familiar? Not that anybody ever asked me to go to college. That part wasn't in the cards for me."

"Why don't we stick to the drinking. You want to know what we were up to Friday?"

I guess he'd made arrangements to take a longer break. When the whistle blew, this woman nodded to my dad, smiled at me, and took his place at the machine. We moved out of her way.

"Not particularly, no. I heard you and your buddies

want to change the drinking age."

"That's part of it."

"You won't change it. The only thing you got the chance to change is your life."

"I'll try it after you do."

We both had to talk louder now that the machines were going again. I'm not sure he heard what I had just said.

"Why are you so against college? You're smart enough, you might be able to get some financial help. Your mother and me—"

"I don't want to go. I'm sick of school anyway."

"Right. You're sick of school but you'd get arrested just to do a school project. Next year, mark my words, you'll be a fish out of water."

"Maybe I'll be a fish *in* water. Just like my daddy. Maybe I'll stay in Salmon Falls the rest of my life."

"Your mother'd like that, I'm sure. What, you think she couldn't manage without you?"

"She'd do just fine," I said, trying to stare him down.

"She always has," he said. I didn't like the way he laughed. "This is just more spite, Kyle. You spite me, you spite your own brains, you even spite your friends. College is fine for them guys, but not for old Kyle. He's gonna grow old and die in Salmon Falls."

I gave him the same sarcastic laugh he'd used about my mother.

"Used to be a guy worked here said he'd never cheat on his wife because nowadays that was just about expected of a guy and he refused to give anybody the satisfaction. I guess he planned to be faithful out of spite."

"I would've liked to meet him."

"I bet you would've. You know what else I bet? I bet he's working on his third divorce right now. You can't be faithful out of spite. You can only be faithful to something if you love it, whether it's your wife, or where you live, or what have you. And I'm not sure you love anything right now."

"I love my mother," I said. "I love my friends."

He'd already turned to walk away when I said, "And I love you."

That was to spite myself.

6

I DON'T GO THERE AS MUCH AS I USED TO OR AS MUCH AS
I should or as much as someday when they're dead
I'll wish I had gone, but once in a while, especially
when I can't get in the mood to go anywhere else, I'll
walk or drive up the hill behind the old Salmon Falls
railroad station—now half bank and half lawyer's
office—and have a visit with Michael and Hermeena
Guenther. After a day like the one I'd just had, I
couldn't think of a better place to go. I headed
straight there after I left the mill.

Michael and Hermeena aren't like regular
friends—they're both old enough to have great-grand-
children, which they do. They're not relatives of mine
either. I'm not really sure what to call them. Michael
was once a painter, and still is, I guess, a picture
painter not a house painter, though he's done some of
the other kind also, and I have helped him do it.

I first met Michael and Hermeena when I was in the fifth grade and thought it would be a great idea to have a paper route. One day when I was pitching papers into driveways, I saw Michael do something like a sideways belly flop into the center of a gigantic snowball bush. Actually I didn't see the belly flop itself, just the before and after. He was barbering the bush with a hedge clipper while standing halfway up a stepladder, and I might have seen the accident coming when he leaned a little too far out to get at the center of the bush. The ladder wobbled for a few seconds, but he seemed to know just how to move with it, so I found myself thinking that the old guy could've almost managed a skateboard, and maybe— you know how kids can get off imagining these things—with his long white hair and his leathery face he was some kind of surfer dude or rodeo rider in the old days, when suddenly, just as I looked away and got ready to pedal my bike again, I heard the ladder whack the ground. When I looked back, there was no sign of Michael except for a snowball bush that looked like it had hiccups.

I let my bike drop, sack of papers and all, and went flying over to the bush. Michael was conscious but shaken up and a bit scratched up too from getting poked in the face by some dead stalks on his way down. Those same stalks were no more help to him than the green ones when he grabbed hold and tried to get himself up off the ground, only to fall back a couple of times, so the snowball bush sounded like a campfire crackling all around him.

That's what I saw when I came to the edge of the bush, and I don't think I'll ever forget the way he looked when he noticed me with my hand reached out to him, how his face changed in a split second from somebody mad at the whole world to somebody so happy he could have kissed me. He immediately grabbed hold of my hand, almost before I had a chance to brace my legs to keep from falling right on top of him, and he went, "Oh, you blessed boy."

I suppose I remember that day so clearly because Michael always gets the same expression on his face whenever he opens the door and sees that it's me. Today was no different.

"Kyle, Kyle, do come in."

And the same with Hermeena, who was instantly at his elbow just as she had appeared out of nowhere that afternoon in a bunch of scarves and bracelets that made her look to me like a Gypsy, only now she cried, "What a wonderful surprise!" whereas then she had been crying, really crying, "You fell, didn't you? He fell in that bush, didn't he? If you try to paint this house all by yourself, Michael Guenther, I'll burn it down, I swear."

Two lemonades later I'd become Michael's answer to fire prevention. I started work as soon as school let out for summer.

Going into their house always brought that first visit back to me, which had been something like walking into a magic pumpkin or a gingerbread house in one of those stories you read as a kid. Outside, Michael and Hermeena's house looked like a lot of the other weather-beaten old houses in Salmon Falls, those semispooky jobs with a big front porch, a small turret on the side, and a couple of dormers up above that guys like my father will sometimes drive by and say, "I'm glad I don't have to paint it." But inside, it was different from any house I'd ever seen. For one thing it was loaded with books, easily as many books as you'd find in one of the smaller town libraries around here. There were also statues, masks, kites, drums, and a small pipe organ, not to mention paintings all over the walls, more than one being of a woman with few or no clothes on. I can remember taking my first look around and thinking, "Whoa."

Michael and Hermeena must like their memories of those days too, because ever since my sophomore year when I stopped working for them, because my after-school and weekend time was getting too busy and my money needs too great, they've done this little ritual whenever I stop by.

First they ask if I want any lemonade, because that's what I drank all the time during the summer. Hermeena will always bring it in a wineglass, the same way she served it back then when I'd take a break from cutting the lawn or raking up leaves to join Michael for his afternoon glass of wine. Even if he wasn't working outside with me on a particular day, he'd come and find me so we could "take some refreshment in the wine garden."

That was usually where he would ask me, like he asked me today, what good movies I'd seen recently.

"Probably nothing you'd like to see," I said, holding back a smile.

"Try me," he said. "I have eclectic tastes. As you should know."

When I was a kid, we must have spent hours talking about movies, and that had worked sort of like a ritual too. I'd keep asking him if he'd seen this or that science-fiction or martial-arts video, and he'd say "No, Kyle, I don't believe I know that one." He was always trying to get me to express my opinion. It was almost like being with a teacher, except he wasn't one, and in fact he never even finished college.

Completely serious, he'd say, "Now in your opinion, Kyle, which is the better film, the *Terminator One* or the *Terminator Two*?" It was always me who would say I should get back to work, never him. A couple of times when it started raining or when Hermeena announced it was too hot to be painting houses, they'd send me downstreet to rent a movie to watch with them. I laugh now at the stuff I used to put them through.

"I think they're the type of people who'd go for something a little more cultured, honey," my mom said one day when I told her what we'd been watching.

To tell you the truth, she hurt my feelings, though she hadn't meant to.

I remember going to the video place the very next day and asking for "a more cultured-type movie, maybe one that an artist might go for" like I was shopping for a Father's Day present or something. "According to what's written on the box, this one here's actually about a painter. It's supposed to be true, too," the man had said, and I showed up at Michael and Hermeena's house that evening feeling like a guy going out to dinner with an engagement ring in his pocket. What felt like a hundred hours later I was fighting with all my might to keep my eyes open.

"You guys remember that foreign movie I picked out that time?"

"That was one of the sweetest things you ever did," Hermeena said, handing me my glass of lemonade. "Which means it was very sweet indeed."

"I remember that movie as if I'd seen it yesterday," Michael said.

"All I remember, Mike, was some naked lady going to the bathroom in a little pot and some lunatic trying to cut off his own ear."

Actually I remembered one more thing, which was waking up with a blanket over the front of me and my head on Michael's shoulder. He was practically asleep too, but by then the movie was over and David Letterman was on. I felt pretty stupid.

Mom used to say that Michael and Hermeena were getting me ready for the day when my parents would be old and my grandparents older still. My dad said that "strange as they are," they were teaching me the value of hard work. Maybe there's something to both ideas, but in my opinion what they really did was get me ready for having different types of friends. In some ways they were my training camp for a guy like Quaker Oats.

"Oh dear. You leave me at a loss," Michael said. "What person your age, these days especially, ever asks a man as old as me for advice?"

"Well, Mike, let's see. Maybe somebody who can't seem to work up the guts to tell a girl he's known for practically half his life what he really feels about her. Or maybe somebody who gets himself involved in a mess like I just got involved in last weekend. When you first heard about it, did you think I'd gone nuts?"

It was just the two of us sitting at the kitchen table. Hermeena had taken a walk downstreet to pick up something for supper. Otherwise I might not have gotten into all this.

"No, Kyle, I didn't. I thought, this is the kind of brave and thoughtful activity that Kyle would be involved in. I just hope he's being careful—I thought that too."

"My father's using it as an excuse to start up on college again."

"Maybe you should listen to your father."

"But you didn't finish, right?"

"No, but I started. I tried it before I laid it aside. And by that time I knew what I wanted to do with my life, which was to paint. You're still finding out what you want to do. You don't want to close any doors."

"Never mind the future," I said. "I need a plan for right now."

"Are you talking about the basketball beauty

or the Beer Rebellion?"

"Either one. I don't know what to do with either one."

He scratched his chin. He has a great head, all craggy-faced with longish, wild white hair like the Ghost of Christmas Past. He took a deep breath.

"You know, the thing about advice is, one should always keep it very simple. I need to think about this."

I had an idea he planned to think till the next time I came over. We sat at the kitchen table and shot the breeze for a while, then Hermeena came back and asked if I'd like to stay for supper. I checked in with Mom and she said fine, not before asking if I'd gone to see my dad. I said I'd tell her all about it when I got home.

As soon as I hung up, Michael said, "Kyle, wait for me out in the wine garden, will you? I think it's warm enough for two hardy souls such as ourselves to stand a few moments outdoors, don't you?"

"No problem," I said.

The wine garden is really nothing more than a majorly cracked cement patio behind the house. Over the years I helped Michael plant flowers around it and cart statues of nymphs and saints out to it, and build an arbor out of cedar poles where he's somehow managed to grow grapevines but never many grapes. The snow was melted all the way to the lawn by now, and the patio itself had dried out in the warmer weather. He'd even pulled the black plastic off one of his statues—probably the way some people take off their shirts or their snow tires, hoping for an early spring. It certainly looked like early spring out there, which is never a pretty sight. I'm referring to piles of dog crap exposed on the lawn and completely brown Christmas trees stuck into the flea-infested snow and mangled gutters hanging off the backs of people's houses from when the ice on their roofs has come avalanching down.

The back door opened, and Michael appeared wearing a jacket and cap and carrying a tray, which he placed on the wrought-iron table between us. (He's the only guy I know who can look cool in a hat with earflaps.) On the tray were two wineglasses and a bottle of wine. He'd forgotten my lemonade.

"Kyle, I've thought as best as I can, and I don't think I can advise you or that my advice will be worth much if I do. I'm sorry. I'm deeply flattered that you should ask."

"That's okay—"

"So I've decided to toast you instead."

He poured a splash of red wine into each glass and handed one to me.

"I'd like to drink this toast to Kyle, my friend, a young man whose life is of supreme importance."

We touched glasses and drank. There were hardly three good swallows in either glass, but we didn't hurry. Basically, I took a sip whenever he did. It was pretty sour stuff. We stood there looking out at the scenery, which we'd done many times together over the past eight years. Now that I was older and more educated, I was supposed to know how out of place Michael's wine garden looked in those narrow backyards, how homesick his little Roman goddess must have felt next to tarp-covered snowmobiles and the hillbilly ice-fishing shack just hauled in off the pond. When I was a kid, though, these things never would have looked strange together. They were all just parts of the place where I lived.

7

"THE WORLD NEEDS YOUNG IDEALISTS."

That's what the judge decided to say to the Salmon Falls Seven—Quake, Diana, Shannon, Condor, a guy named Ethan Damon, his girlfriend, Cathy Starr, and me—all the people left at Stevie's after everybody else had run away.

Then he said that young idealists need to understand the limits that are called laws. Assuming we were "as much the victims as the instigators of a situation that got way out of hand," he would dismiss all charges "this time." But he went on to say, "Any subsequent incidents of this kind will meet with a very different response, I can assure you."

Quake told him straight out that he couldn't promise there'd be no subsequent incidents.

"No one has asked you for such a promise, young man," the judge said. "I just hope you understand *my* promise to you."

Quake said that he did, and the rest of us nodded or mumbled to show that we also understood. Personally, I thought Quake was being a little too what David would call "smart."

But when a group of us got together over at Quake's house afterward, including a few who'd run away from the party when things had gotten hot, Quake said, "We made some mistakes.

"For one thing, our party was too artificial. Anything we do that's going to mean something is going to have to happen at a real party, not some show we stage. Ours got crashed—but that's because we should have been the crashers."

"But what difference does it make if we do civil disobedience at some party where everybody's breaking the law to begin with?" Diana said.

"You don't do stuff like that at parties anyway," Condor said. "It's two completely different things."

"Right. A party's a social occasion, so we do social disobedience," Quake said. "We obey the law where we're expected to break it. We don't drink. If we have the guts for that, then maybe we can take the next step."

Condor gave this noisy sigh for Diana's benefit, but Quake either didn't notice or didn't care. He was on one of his rolls now.

"The thing is, people don't even know what the rebellion is all about. Our own peers don't, really. So we have that to work on too. But people are going to read about us in court for drinking and it's going to be, like, 'What else is new?' Area Teens Caught Drinking—big deal. We've got to establish ourselves in people's minds so that when we do something that goes over the line, people will say, 'We know those kids. They're not troublemakers. So why are they making trouble now?'"

We came up with two new actions, one having to do with our appearance at a party in two weeks, the other with bottle-picking a stretch of road north of Salmon Falls.

Vermont is one of those states with a five-cent deposit on containers of beer and soda, which I guess along with helping the environment works to give some peace of mind to the jerks who toss the containers out their windows as well as some extra income to the poor slobs who go around picking them up. There are even little businesses called redemption centers that do nothing else but take the empties, pay the deposits, and live on the profit left over. One guy I know says that when he first moved up here, his mom thought one of them was some Bible-banger church. They lived here a year before she realized that redemption in Vermont refers to bottles and cans, not people.

"But what's this supposed to prove, Quake?" Shannon asked. I could tell she wasn't too keen on picking up bottles. Bottle drives, where some organization like student council or yearbook goes around to different houses picking up people's empties, was one thing, but scouring the roadsides like somebody on welfare or too proud to take it was something else.

"You sound like that reporter," I said to her. "'What's this supposed to prove?'"

"It doesn't prove anything," Quake said, "but it shows, number one, that we're civic-minded civil resisters, and number two, it shows the connection"—he couldn't stay seated for this one—"between drinking excessively and waste. It's all about waste, isn't it? Wasted brain cells, wasted lives—waste along the roadside. Wasted money even. Pure waste."

"Pure excrement," Condor said, nodding solemnly.

"Plus it'll be fun for us." A few snorts to that one. "No, really. We need something to raise our spirits. It'll be like . . . beach-combing. In fact, that's what we'll do. We'll wear beach clothes. Listen to beach music—"

"It's too cold for beach clothes," Shannon said.

"For a bathing suit, yeah, but we can wear shorts, you know, and surfer shirts, bring a couple of blankets—"

"We could bring some beer and throw the cans into the ditch and then pick them up," I said.

"Recycle in a fraction of the time," Diana said.

"I think that would defeat the purpose," Quake said.

In the early spring just about any stretch of well-traveled road around here is fairly ripe for cans and bottles, because the snow's melting and everything that's gotten tossed from a vehicle since last November has melted down to the soggy matted grass—"like shells upon the shore," Quake said. We chose a stretch of road that ran north out of town in a generally Canadian direction and was the main route to the border before they built the interstate. In fact, Stevie Bouchard had had his fatal accident there, so it was like his ghost was with us once again.

There were nine of us: the core group of Shannon, Diana, Quake, and me plus two guys and three girls who'd been with us at the first action. When I'd heard Diana urging Condor to come along, I'd gone and asked Jennifer Burch if she'd like to join us too. To my great relief both of them said they were too busy, which I took to mean too cool.

Quake insisted that we have signs, as if nine of us in beach clothes walking around in March wasn't conspicuous enough. He'd painted a big one that read:

BOTTLE-PICKIN' BEACH PARTY
(FIGHT THE WASTE!)
WILLOUGHBY H.S. S.U.D.S.
STUDENTS UNDERMINING A DRUNK SOCIETY

and two others that read:

SLOW! BEACHCOMBERS AHEAD

with a picture of a shell in one corner and a beer can in another. I wasn't sure anybody driving by would get this stuff, but there comes a point in Quake's enthusiasms where either you don't have the heart or else you've lost the energy to give him a hard time. We staked out our "section of shore" at ten o'clock Saturday morning, set Shannon's boom box on a car roof, and to the classic California sound of *The Beach Boys' Greatest Hits*, circa 1000 B.C., we fanned out with our garbage bags.

I didn't really own much in the way of certifiable beach wear, but I had on this somewhat ridiculous sombrero that my mom had brought back from a trip

138

to Mexico years ago, plus cutoffs and of course dark shades, which can usually leech the dweeb quality out of most dumb outfits. Quake was fairly subdued for Quake, with a rolled-down sailor hat, round hippie shades, and a long white bathrobe over his shorts and T-shirt. Actually he looked more like an escaped mental patient than a beach bum, but when I told him so, he accused me of splitting hairs.

It was no surprise to me that most of the girls wore bathing suits, though only with the top halves showing—but even so, every breeze rippling across the pools of snowmelt raised goose bumps on their pale arms and got them doing that shoulders-hunched, arms-folded-tight-under-the-boobs thing girls do whenever they haven't dressed right for the weather. Most of the girls I know are as crazy to get a tan as a lot of my guy friends are to get a deer, and in a climate like ours the girls probably have the tougher job.

Diana had worn a bathing suit too, though as usual her getup was a bit different. She'd put on one of her father's gigantic white shirts over it, with the top and bottom buttons undone, plus these long pink tube socks that went above the knee so all that was really bare besides her face was a bit of her chest and some of her thighs, which already looked tan because her skin is naturally dark and the white made it stand out even more. In the same way, her dark glasses made her mouth more noticeable—almost more sexy when she smiled. The thought of her looking like this when she and Condor would go swimming at some lake this summer was too depressing to keep in my mind for more than a minute. I couldn't resist pointing out the fact that he was missing today.

"Saturdays are really busy for him," she said.

"Unlike for the rest of us, right?"

She gave me this funny look that wasn't easy to read with her sunglasses on.

"He's trying to get some stuff done so he can help my dad boil sap tomorrow."

Right then one of two guys picking several yards behind us called out, "We just found some evidence of safe sex over here. This belong to anybody?"

Shannon hurried by us shouting, "Don't! I don't even want to look at that thing." She was wearing two of the hundred rubber gloves that her mother, a nurse, had sent along for our benefit.

"Yeah, but you're the only one who's got the gloves on," called one of the guys as he chased after her. She yelled to Quake that she was going to go home "if Ethan doesn't quit it."

"Come on, guys," Quake said. "Let's remember our purpose here. This is serious."

When he tightened the belt on his bathrobe with

an annoyed tug, Diana and I went shoulder to shoulder, laughing so hard we had tears.

Then we grabbed a couple of empty plastic bags, and pretending they were butterfly nets, we chased him half a mile down the road. Not even Diana could catch him, though.

By noon we had worked our way over to a turnoff Quake had discovered during his pretend dash from the psychiatric ward. It was on a dirt road that crossed the highway, just over a rusted railroad track that ran parallel to the blacktop. It must have been the location of quite a few tailgate parties, because we picked up more cans and bottles there in five minutes than we'd found all morning. Quake decided that we should eat our lunch in that very same spot, which he said would "claim it for the Rebellion." So a couple of us sprinted back for the cars we'd left parked on the shoulder of the main road and zoomed them over to the turnoff. No sooner had we rinsed our hands in some brook water and taken out our cooler of food than we had a visitor.

He came walking around the bend and down a washboard section of road that rose up beyond the turnoff. Shannon was the first to spot him. Diana was the first to call his name.

"David."

He seemed suspicious, like he was about to turn back around, and maybe even a little mad when a few of us jogged up to meet him. He was carrying a bulging grain sack slung over one shoulder.

"Whatcha doing, dude?" I said.

"Not much. What you doing?"

He was in pretty grungy clothes. He looked like he'd spent the morning winching a motor out of a car, which was in fact what he might have been doing. Needless to say, I felt pretty silly in my sombrero.

"We're picking bottles," Quake said. "It's part of the Beer Rebellion."

I gave David a brief smirk, like he and I were above this stuff.

"Want to eat with us, David?" Diana asked. She'd taken off her sunglasses even though we were facing the sun. "You're just in time for lunch."

His face got a little friendlier when he told her, "No time for that. Got work to do. Got to study so my tutor don't raise hell with me."

Then he unshouldered his sack, which rattled like an old Ferris wheel as he set it on the ground right in front of Diana.

"Them's for you, I guess."

He was already turned around and stalking back up the hill by the time Quake had opened the sack and called, "Hey, thanks" after him. I think he would have run after David if I hadn't grabbed his arm.

"That was so sweet," Shannon said. "I feel bad we didn't ask him to come along."

"I didn't think he would've come," Quake said. "Would he have?"

"There must be five dollars' worth of empties in here," Shannon was saying. "I can't believe he did all this for us."

He hadn't. Not to begin with anyway. I could tell he'd been just as surprised to meet us as we'd been to meet him. I bet he even knew about all the cans and bottles dumped at the turnoff—we'd just gotten there before he did. I could almost hear him saying what he always said about "getting set up" someday. "No more math, no more crap from anybody, no more scrounging for the old man."

8

QUAKE INVITED ME, DIANA, AND ANYBODY ELSE FROM
S.U.D.S. who wanted to come along to spend the
weekend sleeping out in his family's mega tree
house. His idea was that some extra time together
would give us more spirit for when we crashed Cindy
Bouvier's party on Saturday with the double resolu-
tion of not drinking a drop and of having a good time
even if it (or somebody else at the party) killed us.
The crash part turned out to be pretty bogus because
I was invited anyway, along with Diana of course,
and we asked Cindy if Quake and a couple other
people could come. Cindy was always reasonable
about stuff like that, and I wondered if the fact of us
having been in court and written up in the local
papers didn't boost our status somewhat. Anyway,
she said, "Why not?"

Diana came over to Quake's Friday afternoon to

help us set everything up, but she was going out that night—I assumed with Condor—and would come back later to spend the rest of it with us. Shannon managed to talk her parents into ungrounding her for the night, mainly by dwelling on the alcohol-free aspects of our adventure. Her parents had been pretty upset about the incident at Stevie's. Nobody else came, which sucked, though a few people said they'd back us up at the party.

So basically I was in two awkward positions, half the time feeling like I was Quake's chaperone and the other half feeling like Diana's father, pacing the rough wood floors of the tree house wondering when in heck that girl was coming home. When I saw Shannon and Quake give each other a peck of a kiss, I seriously thought of leaving. Though it was the wrong time of year, I wished I was camping out with David Logan deep in the woods, waiting for the sky to lighten on the opening day of bow season so we could scramble up into our tree stands and wait for our bucks. If he still wasn't talking to me by October, it would be the first fall in six years that we hadn't gone deer hunting. Since it would also be my first fall out of school, and since Quake and Diana would already be several weeks away at college, I'd be pretty bummed out by then. So why was I planning on staying in town?

Say what you want about Quake—he would never let anybody feel left out, even for the sake of a little romance. He made a special point of talking to me, of telling Shannon stories that had me in them, almost like he could sense how lousy I felt. The Beer Rebellion, not to mention high school itself, was getting old for me. I saw my life like Quake's tree house. On the one hand it was a fairly unusual and wonderful job with several different rooms, one of which was even insulated, and a high boardwalk that led out to an observation tower over a beaver pond, and a woodstove and a great picture window with stained glass around the border and other smaller stained glass windows too. But in another way it was ridiculous, a little kid's fantasy with grown-up ambitions, like an eighteen-year-old guy who likes a girl but sits waiting for her up in a tree house like a big dweeb.

"You're home early, sis." She was. It was only a little past nine.

"We just went for dinner. Plus I wanted to get back to you guys. It's so awesome up here."

"It gives us a chance to see the world from your height," Shannon said.

"Not all it's cracked up to be, is it?"

I'd been majorly relieved to hear her knock on the trapdoor, to see her head and shoulders when Quake

146

opened it, and to watch her climb the rest of the way into the room, but in a minute I was feeling just as down as before. I was glad she was back, extremely glad, while at the same time I was annoyed by the thought that she'd come back for me—not because she liked me in any serious way, but because she really did think of me as a brother, and a little brother at that. I almost said, "You should have stayed out longer," but that would have been a big act, and she would have seen right through it.

"You're not going to believe this," she said, and I braced myself. She waited to say more till Quake had finished closing the dampers on the stove.

"That ought to do us for the rest of the night," he said. "So what won't we believe?"

"We're famous. We've fired the shot heard round the world, babes."

She plopped down on one of the mattresses in front of the stove and made a tent out of her long skirt by planting both feet in front of her.

"Come sit by Mémère LaValley and she tells you the story, okay?"

She patted the mattress beside her and looked at me. Quake and Shannon took the other side. She folded an arm around each of her adopted brothers.

"Condor's mom does part-time freelance work for the *Rutland Herald*, and she found out that there's going to be a story in tomorrow's paper about what happened at Stevie's and—this is the good part— about a similar party that was held in Milton, and another in Bennington."

"You're kidding," Quake said.

"Nope. The kids in Bennington didn't get arrested, and I'm not sure they even tried to, but the Milton kids were. Five of them."

"And it's because of us?"

"One kid—Condor couldn't remember where— but he's quoted as saying, 'We're always talking in school about leadership, but those guys up north have shown us what real leadership is.'"

"Are we actually in the article, like our names?"

"Not you, Shan, which is a bummer. They did call us the Salmon Falls Seven, which includes you, of course. But they mentioned Quake, because he spoke so well in court, and me, which probably has more to do with a basketball court than the other court. And they said the whole Beer Rebellion had been 'masterminded' by one Kyle Nelson after a study of Gandhi in Mr. Raymond Whalen's social studies class."

"Oh, for—"

"Whalen's going to have a bird," Shannon said.

"Condor's all put out because there was no mention of him. He goes, 'I'm the one the cops practically had facedown on the ground!' A little ego problem there, you think? Oh yeah, and at this other school, I forget which one, they've started a petition to lower the drinking age, and they plan to take it around the whole state. So what do you think, guys? Is this awesome or what?"

Quake sounded less than his usual revved-up self. "I think that it's a good idea we're going to Cindy's tomorrow night. People are going to obsess on the legal disobedience and forget the social. We need to show that there's a whole other side to this."

My memory of Cindy's party is confused and always will be, though I still have vague impressions of a couple of things.

I remember getting a round of applause when the four of us entered, because a few people had heard of the article by then, though that died down fast enough when Cindy's boyfriend, Lance, called out, "Bring the rebels a beer!" and Quake announced that we weren't having any beer. I remember Lance giving me the eye, like, "Is this for real?" and me answering with a lamer nod of the head than a real rebel would have given.

Condor was there, of course, and I remember him well. He came up to me with a beer in each hand, and for the rest of the night he made a big point of asking me and Quake too if we wanted one and of saying umpteen thousand times, "This is supposed to be a party."

It wasn't even ten o'clock, and he was wasted. He got so clingy with Diana that a couple of times I saw her push him away, once when he tried to do his head-in-the-lap routine. Then he'd sulk and make these insulted gestures, like, "If that's the way you want it, honey," and then a few minutes later he'd be right back again with not much from Diana that I could see to discourage him, until he really got on her nerves.

I wanted to go talk to her, but just like at the last party, the one at Jennifer's, something or somebody always kept getting in the way. First I found myself listening to this totally sickening bit from Shannon about Quake's various preoccupations and how she wasn't sure whether he'd ever be ready for a committed relationship. Finally, even though Shannon is one of the last people in the world I'd ever want to hurt, I just had to tell her that number one, I wasn't interested, and number two, I didn't appreciate sitting through her or anybody else's analysis of my best friend.

That got rid of her in a hurry, but I was really out in the open then. Diana was still involved in negotiating access to her personal space, Quake was off amusing himself and some other people too with his classic impersonation of a sore thumb, and everybody else was doing what you normally do at a party, which is have a good time.

That's when Jennifer Burch came over, no small amount of buzzed herself, and told me, "You look like the saddest poor baby in the world." And she looked like the sexiest rich baby, all tan in her short skirt and tank top from a family vacation in Florida. It was starting to feel like the party at her A-frame all over again. If I'd been drinking, I'd have sworn the strange sensation came from being drunk.

This time, though—and I'm not sure who made the first move—the two of us started getting into it pretty heavy. There were a couple of bedrooms off the living room, at least one of which was in urgent use right then, and I have no doubt that if things had gone on for much longer, I would have had Jennifer—or maybe I should say she would have had me—in the other one. As it was, I had my hands in places where I'm not in the habit of having my hands when people are watching me. She did too. And even though she felt so incredibly good to me, like a clean bed feels after fourteen hours of tramping through the woods, and though I really wanted her, I felt pretty depressed too, because for one thing she was drunk and I wasn't, and for another here she was just about screaming to me and the whole world that she was hot for me when I couldn't even kiss her without planning the next move that would give me another glimpse of Diana. To me you don't get much lower than loving up somebody you don't even care about, but there we were, or I should say there I was, because I think Jennifer cared about me quite a bit.

I got her off my lap, though, and told her to wait for me when I saw Diana talking to Quake with Condor in tow behind her looking so shit-faced he could barely stand. At first I wondered if she wasn't breaking up some confrontation between them—another repeat from February, with Quake the target this time instead of David—in which case I was going to give C.C. the sock in the head that I should have given him back then. I didn't care that he was drunk, I didn't get him drunk. Screw him.

But when I got over to Diana, I realized she was asking Quake to help her get Condor to her car so she could drive him home. Quake was all set to go, but I changed his plan with such a bossy voice that it struck even me as ridiculous.

"I'll do it," I snapped.

"Never mind, Kyle," Diana said, looking like she was disgusted with the whole bunch of us. "You're busy."

"I'm not busy," I said.

"I'm not going home," Condor said.

I turned to Quake. "Let me, okay? This may not be the best job for a pacifist."

Actually, though, once Diana and I had each put an arm around Condor, and after he'd managed to wave his good-byes like a wounded general being carried off the battlefield, he became so friendly he was almost disgusting.

"You're all right, Kyle, you know that? If I was a girl, I'd go out with you."

"Appreciate it. Let's all head for the car, okay?"

"You know what I like about you, Kyle? You get along with everybody. Nerds, rednecks, it doesn't matter because you're a genuine human being. I wouldn't say this to anybody, but except for Wonder Woman here, you're about the only person in this stinking Appalachian shithouse I can stand."

It took him about three minutes and four tries just to get that little speech out of his mouth. We folded him into the passenger seat of Diana's Subaru, and after he'd held her face down to his for an additional three minutes' worth of apologies and kisses and what I could only imagine to be unbearable lower-back pain, Diana managed to get loose, straighten up, and shut the door.

"Thanks, Kyle," she said.

I followed her around to the back of the car. "I can drive him," I said.

"No," she called with her back to me. "He'll only go with me. Quake already offered."

"Diana, talk to me for a minute, will you?"

"What?" she said, turning around. Then more softly, "What?"

"Why do you waste your time with somebody like him?"

"Who else should I waste it with, Kyle?"

"How about somebody decent? You could have any guy you wanted."

"Uh-huh . . ."

Just then Condor started hollering through the closed window. Diana said "Just a minute" to me and went to tell him she had to talk to me and would be back soon. He insisted on rolling down the window and kissing her before she could leave.

"So . . ." she said when she'd joined me at the rear of the car again.

"So, you remember my question?"

She nodded, biting one of her fingernails.

"Ever seen a prom picture, Kyle?"

"I would think so. What's that got to do with anything?"

"How many have you seen where the girl's taller than the guy?"

"Yours for one." She'd gone to the prom last year with a guy a grade ahead of us who was a basketball player too, but still not as tall as Diana. "And you looked terrific, by the way."

"You're nice to say so. It took an entire day and cost almost three hundred dollars for me to get ready for that one night. My dad said no matter what it cost . . . he wanted me to feel like a queen. And you know what everybody said when they saw the picture? 'Diana is such a tall girl, isn't she?'"

"So what? So . . . the guy was short. Condor ain't that much taller than me as far as that goes."

"The problem isn't that the guys are short, Kyle. The problem is that they're small. They see a girl who's taller than them or a better athlete than them and they get even smaller. They shrink to nothing. So yeah, Condor's got some problems, and I know them better than you do. But you know what? He doesn't see me as a good friend, or a good basketball player, or a lovable giant, or a nice piece of affirmative action because I have a three-point-nine-nine-nine-whatever plus a quarter pint of real Indian blood—you know? He sees me as just a girl he likes, and you have no idea how good it feels to be seen that way."

"I could make you feel that way too."

She looked away from me. "It looks like you already have your hands full. What would Jennifer say?"

"Jennifer's not who I care about." No turning

back now. "I like you a lot, Diana, and not just like a sister either. Why don't we go out or something. Let's just try it, huh? I haven't got all my growth yet, you know."

She started to smile. She touched my cheek. "Call me," she said.

She turned and began walking around to the driver's side.

"Yes or no, Diana." I grabbed her arm. "Yes or no. I don't want to wait. Tell me now."

"Yes," she said.

I was twelve feet tall.

"But call me."

I couldn't believe that Diana would have called my mom to give her the good news, but I was high enough that night to believe anything. Maybe she had just called to talk to me, and the words had slipped out in conversation. I couldn't think of any other reason why my mom would've sprung off the porch and thrown her arms around me as soon as Quake stopped to let me out of the car. I was all set to treat the whole thing lightly, you know, nothing more than what a savvy guy will do when he's good and ready, but then I felt her sobbing in my arms.

"Mom?"

She let out a horrible wail. I heard Quake kill his

engine and get out of the car.

"We all okay here?" he said, still standing by his door.

"I was so sure it was you." My mother was crying. "I was so sure."

"It is me. Of course it's me. What's wrong, Mom?"

"I just knew you were in that car. Oh dear God."

She pulled back from me without letting go and turned her head just as a pair of headlights lit up the side of the house.

"He's all right!" she shouted toward the car. "It's him!" Then to me: "It's your father. He was coming to pick me up."

All of a sudden it was like a dream, like I was a little boy again, with my mother and father squeezing me at the same time. I saw Quake standing there with his face hanging out—and I almost worried he was going to fade out of the dream as their hold on me got tighter and tighter, and right away I knew for sure that I didn't want him to. My father was groaning in my ear.

"What's wrong?" I yelled.

"There was an accident," my mother said. "Your father heard it on the CB. We thought sure you were in the car."

"Where was this?" Quake said.

"Down on Twilight Road," my father said, "where it goes under the interstate."

"Your friends," my mother was crying, "your poor friends."

"What?" I said, yanking away from her. "Who was it?"

"Are they hurt badly?"—it was Quake, standing next to me now.

"They don't know if the boy will make it," my dad said, to Quake, not me.

"They didn't say who it was!" my mother cried. "That's what had us so frantic. They just kept saying a boy, a boy, a red Subaru, and the EMTs were having a hard time getting them out because the girl . . . was so big."

She looked like she was going to fold up and collapse right in front of me. I turned to Quake—he was giving out too.

"Honey. Honey . . ." My mother was reaching out to me, but I was backing away. It was my dad who said, "She didn't suffer, son."

3

PART

1

IT'S ONLY BECAUSE A LITTLE TIME HAS PASSED THAT I
can even talk about the days after Diana died. Not all
the things that happened then were awful, but most
of them were awful. I'll probably never live through
anything so awful.

Basically the whole school just went to pieces.
Because this is a small-town place where news trav-
els fast, most of the kids knew what had happened by
the time Monday rolled around, but there were a few
who didn't, so the first hours of school were like
sweeping a minefield to set off the unexploded
mines. You'd walk softly down the hall just thinking
to yourself where you had to go and how long before
you could get there, and then there'd be this horrible
explosion of crying at a locker or inside a classroom.
People were either tearing by you with their faces all
a mess heading for the bathroom or the guidance

office, or else drifting like zombies down the hall.

You couldn't be anywhere, sit down anywhere, not the cafeteria, not study hall, not some special assembly on "the tragic events of this past weekend," without somebody storming out of it in tears— usually two girls, with one out of control and the other acting as her attendant, sometimes a girl and a guy, with the guy always acting as the attendant. As far as I could tell, everybody was acting to some extent. Probably I was too.

A lot of people took to wearing sunglasses indoors, so it sometimes felt like we were in Hollywood and everybody's movie had flopped on the same day. You would start laughing all of a sudden at the dumbest thing, and people all around you would be really offended, like how can he be laughing at a time like this, and you actually wanted to offend them because you were positive that no one could have loved Diana as much as you had, but then just like that you'd be crying, and people would have their arms around you. That may be what I remember most, the constant hugging every minute. I can't have somebody my own age hug me even now without feeling like Diana's just died all over again.

After the first forty-eight hours it was pretty certain that Condor would live but not real certain how well.

That put him right in the center ring of the big circus that was coming to town hour by hour, even though he was still in an intensive care unit twenty-five miles away. Kids our age are always blaming people and always feeling sorry for people, mostly themselves, but now Condor had become the ultimate pity object and the ultimate blame object all in one mangled body, though some people had trouble sorting out which they felt more and which he deserved more. I was not one of those people.

Nobody except Condor knew exactly how the accident had happened, but of course he'd been drunk—they determined that in the emergency room—so he had no responsibility for remembering what had happened or even for anything he'd done to make it happen. There was one other witness, a guy who'd been behind their car for a few minutes on the interstate and who was the first person to arrive at the accident on Twilight Road. He told the cops he'd seen "what looked like a struggle" going on in a car up ahead of him. He'd pulled closer and flashed his high beams. What he saw then "looked like a couple necking." They'd separated, he'd switched down his lights and let up on his speed, feeling a little too nosey, I guess, while the other car accelerated, and then the distance between them grew. Soon after he'd gotten off the interstate, he came upon the same car folded up against a bridge abutment on the under-pass. At first he thought the passenger must have gotten out of the car or been thrown from the car. That's because the passenger's head was lying in the driver's lap. Whether he'd been that way before the accident or fallen that way on impact, nobody knew.

I knew.

In either case, the girl's knees had absorbed a good deal of the impact before it reached the boy's head. She'd likely have lost both legs had she lived.

My closest friends all dealt with the death in their own ways. One way Shannon dealt with it was by refusing to talk to me. It was like me brushing her off at the party and Diana getting killed after it were connected in some weird way that she couldn't explain and didn't have to. Jennifer, on the other hand, was never far out of sight, or reach. I noticed she always made a point of telling people that I had been Diana's best and truest friend. I guess if that was the case, it made her like the First Lady of Grief. She'd take my arm like first ladies do and stare the public bravely in the face.

Quake is the hardest one to pin down and describe because, I think, he was the one who strug-gled the most with his feelings. Most of us had our places in the game plan pretty well figured out by the time of the funeral. I was into my own personal certainty of what had happened to Diana, Shannon was into taking offense at everything, and Jennifer was into healing the world's pain in general and mine in particular. Quake was just into the pain itself, I guess, with the difference being that he didn't want to be into it, he just was. He cried a few times at first, but then he just kept everything inside. He never cut loose in his old zany way. He became extra studious, making things hard that had always come easy to him. He went from being one of the world's champion talkers to being a man of few words.

Which brings us to David Logan, who quit his silent treatment long enough to ask, "Why did you let her get into the car with a guy that drunk?"

I shoved him away from me so hard, I was sure we would end up in a fight. Looking back, I wonder if I almost wanted him to kick the crap out of me.

"You would've handled it, right, Dave? You would've known just what to do. Diana looked after your ass, David; you didn't take care of her. You would've been as clueless as you always are."

Instead of pounding on me, though, he just held up both his hands and took a step back.

"Hey, dude, nobody's blaming you. I just thought you would have had a reason, that's all."

The same day, and without giving a reason, David

dropped out of school. He was one math and a half credit of English away from his diploma.

Diana's parents had decided, maybe with some help from all the counselors who were crawling all over us like bugs, that her friends should have some part in planning her funeral. It was a big mistake, I think.

A bunch of us met at my house to decide what recorded song we'd play to balance out the hymns and stuff that wouldn't mean so much to people our age. There were about ten of us packed into our kitchen, which could seem crowded with just one other person besides my mom and me, but that was the usual scene during the time before and after the funeral: people packed into one room or another of some kid's house. You could go to any kid's house you wanted, and except for handling explosives or maybe drinking you could do anything you wanted, stay as long as you wanted, sleep there, shower there—the only thing parents would do is go down-street or into town when they ran out of soda or soap and tell you to call your parents when it got late. Anything to keep us off the road and this side of suicide.

Anyway, we were into this thing about "Candle in the Wind," a song by Elton John, which some kids wanted to be the song that got played at the funeral.

166

The idea was that it had been played a few years back for Lady Diana's funeral and people had called Diana LaValley "Lady Di" as in the princess of basketball, so what song could be better?

"But it's going to be stupid, though," I said. "Everybody thinks of it as Lady Diana's song. So who are they going to be thinking about when we play it? I want them to be thinking about Diana LaValley. Nobody else."

"No, but that's the thing, though, Kyle," said Jennifer, who was a big fan of the idea. "When Lady Di got killed, millions of people all over the world mourned. So it's, like, for us to use this song is saying that's how much she meant to us. She wasn't a famous person but our feelings are just the same as if she was a famous person. You know?"

Cindy Bouvier said, "It would be like that thing we're doing in English where you say something famous and it makes you think . . . Quake, what's that thing?"

"Allusion," he said, with his head resting between his hands. He sounded like he'd just said the word for the thousandth time that day.

"Yeah, like that. Allusion."

"But it was already an allusion," Quake said, still bummed-out-looking but at least making eye contact. "The original words were 'Goodbye Norma

Jean.' That was Marilyn Monroe's real name. Elton John changed it to be about Lady Di."

"But nobody knows that obscure stuff, Quake, except somebody like you," Cindy said.

"Or like they forget," said her boyfriend, Lance. He was standing at the kitchen counter behind us first-string mourners. "Like you guys were talking, and I'm going to myself, Who's Lady Di? I'm serious."

"What do you think, Mrs. Nelson? What's your opinion on the song?" Jennifer said.

My mother had been filling some bowls of chips and mixing up some dip for us to snack on. She still had her back to us when she said, "You guys don't want to hear what I think."

I knew my mom well enough to know that she was giving us one last chance to avoid hearing what she thought, and that sometimes it was a good idea to consider that option. But everybody was immediately into being a good guest and saying "Yes" and "Sure"—even Lance said, "We want to hear it, definitely."

Mom turned around. She didn't look great—she hadn't looked good since the accident. She put two big bowls of chips and a little bowl of dip on the table, she nodded when the kids said thanks, and I thought maybe she wasn't going to say anything. But then she said, "You want to know my opinion, do you?"

Everybody did.

"I think you can play the jingle for the Ty-D-Bol commercial for all it's going to mean. You guys think you own this. Because Diana was *your* friend, so this is all about *your* feelings. Do any of you have the foggiest idea what it's like to wake up at two o'clock in the morning absolutely convinced that your baby has smothered to death in his crib—except he's thirteen now? In five years Diana LaValley won't mean much more to you than the other Diana, but those poor parents . . . will never . . ."

She waved her hand in front of her face and left us alone. "Candle in the Wind" was put to a vote and won unanimously with two abstentions, those being Quake's and mine.

After everybody went home I found Mom in her bedroom sitting on the edge of her bed. She snuffed out her cigarette as soon as she heard me.

"Your old lady's a real bitch, right?"

"Nobody better say it."

"Yeah, but they all think it."

I told her what I thought about anything they might think, and for once I didn't get any flack about the F-word in the house. I sat down beside her, and I rubbed her back, thinking right away how Diana had done the same thing for Mrs. Cantor.

"We're just kids, Mom. We don't have a clue."

"Yeah, that's the point, though, ain't it? You don't need some old lady ragging on you for what you don't understand because you have no way of understanding it. I'm sorry, honey."

"Forget it," I said. I squeezed her shoulder. "We asked you for your opinion, right?"

"Yeah, I guess you did. And, oh boy, am I in the mood to give it these days!"

"So do it," I said. I kept my arm around her.

"That's not always such a good idea. Some of the girls at work—I call them girls, most of them are mothers or old enough to be, some older than me— they were talking the other day about the accident and kids drinking and all. And they're all going, 'We did the same things when we were young.' Like this was some deep observation on life. And I know I hurt some of their feelings, but I couldn't help saying, 'Yeah, but you didn't die when you were young, did you?'"

When I started to cry, she said, "Oh honey, I didn't mean to upset you." She rubbed my neck. I shook my head.

"It's not that," I managed to say.

"Then what is it?"

"I just keep thinking . . . if I'd listened to what you said, and asked Diana out weeks ago, maybe she wouldn't have been with Condor—"

"Shh. Shh. No, no." She shook her head slowly. "You're trying to figure out fate, Kyle. All a person's supposed to figure out is right and wrong. You didn't do anything wrong. You can't let your conscience try to act like a fortune-teller."

She pulled my face against her shoulder. I didn't pull away.

"Maybe there's one boy out there tonight who has something to feel guilty about, but honey, you ain't him."

2

THAT OTHER BOY SUPPOSEDLY DID FEEL GUILTY,
terribly guilty, but according to his own version of
the facts. Again and again people would hear Condor
say that if only he hadn't been so drunk that night
Diana wouldn't have had to drive him home. That
became the official mistake, the official guilt. He'd
gotten drunk, she'd driven him home. Not that he'd
been all over her in the car so much she couldn't
drive. Not that he'd given some guy on the road the
false impression that Diana was making out while
she was driving, which some people now actually
believed, and which is something Diana would never
have done, even with a guy she loved a whole lot,
because she just didn't do stupid things. According to
Reggie Barton, Condor even said the accident wouldn't
have happened if he hadn't been so drunk because he

was a better driver than Diana was. After all, he'd driven in California.

Jennifer talked me into going up to the hospital, which was a must-do thing for practically every kid who wasn't in the hospital himself. Every day at school we heard the latest dispatches from people who'd been bedside the night before. Condor's out of ICU. Condor smiled at a joke. Condor took a sip of a milkshake. Condor said if he hadn't been so drunk . . .

I supposed I could deal with it because there wouldn't be much I'd have to do. Guys our age have it fairly easy when it comes to social visits of a deadly formal or heartbreaking sort. The girls have it pretty much wrapped up. Our job is to drive—unless, of course, we're too drunk to exercise our superior driving skills—to stand behind the girls with our hands on their shoulders and our own shoulders as square as possible, as if to say that if the little boy with leukemia should ever, no matter what time of day or night, need somebody's ass kicked all he has to do is call, we'll be there—and then afterward to get some credit for strength and sensitivity when we take the girls back to the cars.

I was getting quite a bit of credit already from Jennifer, and it was messing up my head in all kinds of ways. I could do no wrong for one thing. A guy might think that's what he wants a girl to believe, but unless his goal in life is to become a world-class jerk, she's never doing him a favor. I think she really cared about me, but deep down I'm not sure we respected each other much. To her I was just some rough-around-the-edges towny from a broken home who now had a broken heart from losing his good friend, who happened to be the most popular girl in the school. I suppose that anything Jennifer could do for me right then would prove to herself that she wasn't a snob or a girl who used guys, like some people said she was, or for that matter a heartless bitch, because I suspect that aside from feeling sorry for me she really felt nothing in her heart for Diana at all except resentment that she was now even more popular dead than she had been alive. I wonder if that bitter, empty feeling didn't scare Jennifer a little.

On my side, I had always thought of Jennifer as this foxy airhead with too much money, though come to find out she was a lot smarter than she let on. She was nice too, nicer than she often got credit for, but there was not much else about her that I admired. And that made me feel like a piece of crap every time I touched her. Not to mention how disloyal I felt to Diana. Even if I'd never asked Diana out, even if I'd never wanted to, what kind of friend was I, carrying on with this girl with Diana not even in her grave? But I didn't want to be alone. With David dropped out of school and Quake going further and further into his shell and Diana never coming back, that's what I would have been without Jennifer. And that, I guess, is what scared me.

When we got to the hospital shortly after dark, it was standing room only, the nurses having let the rules relax in view of the recent tragedy, etc. A few kids as well as a handful of grown-ups were out in the hall, like smokers at a dance, but of course no one was smoking. I could see nothing in the room at first except the backs of people's heads, a few metallic get-well balloons on the ceiling, and a light that rose from where I assumed Condor's head must be. Somebody was crying. I could hear Condor's voice, raspy and faint, though I couldn't make out any words.

When our presence became known, some of the people in front moved back, figuring to give us our turn and maybe hoping to get some distance from whatever little volcano had just erupted bedside.

I admit it did give me a jolt to see Condor with all these cords and pulleys attached to his legs, and half his face bandaged, and his head shaved and a metal halo screwed right into it. His lips were all chapped and gross like an old man's. I wasn't about to cry, and I certainly wasn't about to sit down on the goddamn floor next to his bed like a few of the girls were doing, one of them with her head down on the mattress and Condor's hand in her hair like he was Gandhi giving his deathbed blessing. But I did think how the poor bastard had gotten way more than he'd bargained for and had gotten it in an incredible hurry. It would take him a long time to get rid of it, if he ever did.

The second jolt came when he saw me and started to cry as soon as he'd said my name. At least his face twisted up like he was going to cry. He held out his hand, the one he'd had in Wendy Wylie's hair, and there wasn't too much I could do except go over to the bed. Wendy got up off the floor, with her head still bowed and her long hair hiding her face, to make room.

When I got close enough to take Condor's hand, he locked our thumbs together. His grip wasn't that bad. Then all of a sudden he was pulling me down, and there was no place for my head to go except practically down to his chest unless I wanted to risk banging into his messed-up swollen face, which I certainly didn't.

"We were her guys, man," he said in a loud whisper. "We're the ones she loved."

I felt sick. When I got myself straightened up, I

was really dizzy. It didn't help that I had a flash of Diana straightening up after letting him kiss her from inside her car. When Jennifer put her fingers around my neck, I locked my arm around her, as much to keep my feet as anything else. Then somebody burst into tears on the other side of the bed, a younger girl around junior high age, who I took to be Condor's sister.

After a few pitiful gulps she said, "I know Diana's happy now . . . because she can see you guys together. . . ."

Somebody else stormed out of the room, with a friend rushing out close behind her. Another eruption, this time out in the hall. Hugs, no doubt. Condor's mother stepped from the circle and squeezed her daughter close to her side. She looked like the nicest woman. I guess I'd expected her to look like an older female version of her son. She smiled at me.

"Did you see what they did outside?" she said. "Go see."

Bodies were moving aside once again, and I felt Jennifer ushering me toward the darkened window. Her chin came to rest on my shoulder as she looked over it. Down on the lawn was a long white banner like they put up on the gym wall at basketball games, suspended like a loose volleyball net between two small trees. I could tell there were words on it—every so often the red part of a letter became visible in the glow from a streetlight out in the parking lot. It looked like a bloodstain blowing in the dark.

Jennifer whispered in my ear, "Can you see?"

"It's too dark," I said, turning around. "I can't read it."

Condor's mother looked down at her son, who looked at nobody when she said, "It says, 'We forgive you, C.C. Please forgive yourself.'"

She looked at me and said, "We don't even know who put it there."

She was starting to lose it. Several people said they had "a pretty good idea." I had an even better one. Whoever it was who had painted that banner wasn't lying in a steel drawer somewhere like my sister, Diana.

3

IT WAS JUST ONE THING TO SURVIVE AFTER ANOTHER, and the funeral was the worst. The LaValleys had decided not to have a wake; otherwise that might have been the worst. The funeral made everything so real. Before that everything was like dreaming, and I'm sure that in some part of myself I was still hoping that I'd feel my mom's hand on my shoulder and hear her voice telling me to wake up now or I'd be late for school. The funeral, though, was like having some brute twist your arm behind your back to make you say something you didn't want to say. Diana is dead. Say the words.

The thing was huge. Outside of a fair or something like that, I'd never seen so many cars parked in one place, lining the roads and extending even beyond where the thirty-five-mile-per-hour signs change to fifty. Just the sound of so many silent people sitting down at one time was like God coming into a room. A couple of times I actually had to remind myself to breathe.

They had Diana's long casket in the aisle up in front with a blanket over it that one of her hundreds of Canadian relatives had made and on top of that a great bouquet of roses, which creeped me out for some strange reason. Then I remembered that night of her thousandth point and how Condor had appeared with his big bouquet. I'd have been willing to relive that moment a thousand times to make her alive. If I could have snapped my fingers and changed her funeral to their wedding, I would have done it and given the bride away too. I would have walked up the aisle on my knees, carrying their wedding rings on a little purple cushion.

And that's part of what weighed me down so hard—that there were no deals. Half your life is dealing when you're my age, and if you're good at life you know how to deal, how to make that pitiful plea, do that dirty chore, come up with that irresistible extra-credit project, offer to make that outrageous sacrifice, let me go Friday and I swear to God you can take away my stereo, you can give away my dog, but now all of a terrible sudden there was to be none of that. Diana was dead, and all deals were off.

•   •   •

Quake, Jennifer, and I were able to sit fairly close to the front, not that far behind the Canadians, who whispered in French but cried the same as everybody else. I caught a glimpse of David way in the back, the only time I ever saw him in a tie. My parents both came; all my teachers came. Even Michael and Hermeena came. I think it was when I saw them that I realized that as bad as this was going to be and as awful as it was to see that blanket-covered box set up in the aisle, the part after was going to be even worse, when everybody filed out and went back to their barns, their machines, or their lockers and Diana went back to the funeral home to wait until the ground thawed enough to bury her. We were all together now, like on Noah's Ark but with two of every kind of neighbor instead of animals. I was wishing we could all just sail off to heaven with Diana. I was so, so grateful that at least I'd be seeing Michael and Hermeena after the service.

In between some prayers and stuff like that, the high school chorus sang a song about saying farewell that got a lot of people crying. One of Diana's cousins read a letter from one of Diana's little sisters, Celine, that was written to Diana up in Heaven. Actually, Quake had wanted us to do something from our group that not only praised Diana but also set the record straight once and for all that she had kept her promise not to drink that night. Come to find out, though, more than one every-weekend drinker and, according to some people, even Diana's mother put some of the blame for Diana's accident on her involvement with us. The fact that we'd taken a stand by not drinking that night didn't even get considered. We just were part of that outfit that wanted to lower the drinking age and got busted by the cops for having a drinking party right out in the open. End of story. So we more or less got told that any message from us would not be appropriate.

There were enough messages already, I guess. Half a dozen people got up to say their parts before the priest did. After the cousin got done Celine LaValley's letter, the basketball coach got up to say some things about what a great student athlete Diana had been and how maybe the truly greatest thing about her was the way she always took a special interest in the younger players, even the ones who were likely to spend more of their seasons on the bench than on the court, and that maybe that quality had to do with her being the oldest of seven wonderful children. He also said that the LaValley family and the teachers' association had gotten together to start a scholarship in Diana's name.

Then it was "Candle in the Wind," and even though that got people crying again and served as the soundtrack for at least one dramatic exit—one weeper plus two red-eyed escorts—to me the whole thing sounded so fake and stupid coming over the church PA system that I was ashamed to have had anything to do with it. After the song Cindy Bouvier went up to the podium to read a poem that she'd written and could barely get through.

Diana, you meant something to us all,
Your warm smile, the way that you played
  basketball,
Your good advice to all your friends,
Who can't believe that your life would end.

This is where she started to lose it.

We walk the halls, give hugs, and cry.
Why did such a good person have to die?
People say hello to me and I just nod.
I'm not mad at them, I'm mad at God.
Maybe someday you'll tell us the score,
When we meet you again at Heaven's door.

When the priest did his sermon, he mentioned "the young lady's lovely poem" and said how right she was to say that Diana's death was a mystery with reasons known only to God. Quake had always told me that there was no real disagreement between science and religion, that they just explored different things, but now I said to myself, Quake's wrong. In science everything has a reasonable explanation, whereas in religion, at least as far as I could tell from what I was hearing today, nothing does.

After the funeral I almost punched out a teacher, an ex-teacher to be exact. People were milling around in little groups outside the church waiting for their chance to say one last thing to the family. I wandered over to see Mrs. Cantor, who I knew had taken Diana's death very hard. She was talking with Mr. Whalen and another social studies teacher plus this other guy named Mr. Keller who'd been my English teacher freshman year and then left teaching to write for a magazine or something.

Anyway, when I got up to them, I heard Whalen say, "I'm so glad Father Guyette said that part about the designated driver, that people shouldn't abandon that idea just because of a freak accident. I thought that took some guts. It was important for our kids to hear that."

Mrs. Cantor and the other teacher were nodding—I doubt Mrs. Cantor was up to speaking words at that point—but then this Keller goes, "What would've taken more guts is if he'd said the designated driver idea is a big crock. If one person in a car is drunk, it's drunk driving. But nobody's going to say that because three quarters of the people in a position to say so are drunks themselves."

He saw me then, and I thought he'd clam up, but it was like with me there he was going to go all the way.

"Don't you just love it," he said, "the way they always ask when something like this happens if there was alcohol involved? In this county that's like asking people on the *Titanic* if water was involved. 'Were the kids drinking?' Right? All the drunks want to know if the kids were drinking. Past a certain point it doesn't even matter. The kids are growing up in the bar."

"What's your problem?" I said really loud.

I expected that to shock everybody for a moment, but Keller turned to me like he'd been hoping with all his might for me to ask. I almost wondered if he was drunk himself.

"My problem, young man, is that I'm sick to my stomach and sick to my heart of going to nauseating funerals for people who look like you." He poked his finger right into my chest.

That's when I could have hit him, but to tell you the truth, he looked like a few people had worked him over already. There was almost no point.

Michael had drawn me a sketch and even cut a few stencils before we met at his house after the funeral. Hermeena had gone out and actually bought me a bag of spray paints, six cans in four different colors.

"I feel a little funny doing this," Michael said.

"Not that it's the first time Michael has been involved in the making of graffiti," Hermeena said.

"But that was far away and long ago," he said, sighing.

I asked where and when, not that it was of much interest to me at the time, but he seemed so depressed I wanted to distract him. He just frowned and shook his head, though Hermeena whispered in my ear, "Frankfurt, Germany, 1969. He was a marvel."

Getting help from Michael for painting a memorial to Diana probably had as much to do with my own ego as with my feelings for her. I knew I couldn't draw. Quake could, naturally, and I'd heard that Condor was actually sending a frigging diagram for when we met that night to paint a mural on the bridge abutment where Diana had died. I felt that for once I wasn't going to take a backseat to someone else.

"I appreciate this," I told them. "I'm not sure what's going to get used. A bunch of us are doing it, so we'll probably spend half the night arguing. I'm sure we'll use the paint, though."

"Just be careful, Kyle," Michael said. "The thing today was hard enough. But if ever . . ."

Hermeena patted his neck and said she knew I'd take care. She asked if I wanted a glass of lemonade. I told her I had to run. Michael didn't offer me any wine.

4

FOR THE PAST SEVERAL DAYS PEOPLE HAD BEEN LAYING flowers at the bridge abutment where Diana's car had crashed, that and chucking what must have been two hundred empty beer cans by the time we arrived to paint our mural. Adults and even some kids made like they were shocked beyond all belief by such a tribute, but the same thing had happened three years ago when Stevie Bouchard had gotten killed. Most of the cans were gone from around his barn by now, but after he died you couldn't even go near the place without crushing one or two of them underfoot.

Actually, one of our plans for that night was to clear away all the cans before we put paint on concrete. Quake said we should take them in for deposit and give the money to the scholarship fund. It was pretty depressing work compared to the last time we'd gone picking, when Diana had looked so great in her white shirt and tube socks and had run so fast after Quake when he seemed to be escaping from an insane asylum. No escape tonight. Now we just bagged up the cans, some still dripping beer, and threw the loaded bags into Ethan Damon's pickup. It only took us a few minutes.

I was surprised how many people showed up. Besides Quake and me, there must have been close to twenty other kids there, including Jennifer, who'd driven over with me, plus Shannon, Cindy, Lance, and to my surprise David Logan. It was Shannon's idea to invite him. I wanted to tell her what a good person she was to do it and even to tell David how glad I was to see him there, but none of that would have come out the way I wanted it to. We more or less acknowledged each other, that was all.

David had brought along this air compressor that he'd borrowed from some relative with a shade-tree body shop and enough white paint to cover all the older graffiti and make a clean background on the cement. Quake rigged up his generator to the compressor and to a rack of headlights, but somebody had brought along music, including the "Candle in the Wind" tape, and we couldn't hear the music over the generator (which to my mind argued strongly for the generator), so after David had finished putting the white on the wall, they made

Quake kill the engine and took turns running different cars with the headlights on.

Sure enough, Condor had sent along some sketches, which for some people, mostly a couple of girls that worshiped him, deserved all the respect due to a last will and testament. As it turned out, though, one of his ideas was to have a large pair of legs in basketball sneakers running across the mural, and one of the stencils I'd gotten from Mike was for a very long pair of arms holding a basketball, so it was decided immediately to replace his legs with my arms and fit them into his overall design. People were going, like, Wow, like what an awesome coincidence, even Quake, like how wonderful it was that my picture and Condor's were in the same ballpark, not thinking for even a minute that this same wonderful destiny had put Diana and Condor in the same car.

It was at the bridge that I finally lost it altogether. I guess everything that had been building up inside of me had to come out sometime, and it came out then.

A couple of people were holding up the stencil for one of the arms so I could spray it on when a truck slowed down, honking its horn like crazy, and Reggie Barton called out that we were "doing good work." He laid some rubber taking off, and afterward there was that bubbly little wake of girl giggles and guy guffaws that made us sound like any other party, and it pissed me off more than I could say.

Then when I told Jenn and Cindy to take away the stencil, I saw that some of the paint had run down behind it so that what I'd painted looked like an arm that was melting. It was an easy enough thing to fix, but something about how I was feeling right then and the way Cindy had to shriek, "Oh shit, Kyle, look what happened!" just threw my switch.

I took the can and sprayed a mess all over the arm till you couldn't even see that it had been an arm, and then I started smashing the can on the cement and swearing. Then when it fell out of my hand, which by now was pretty numb from hammering on the bridge, I bent over, grabbed the can, and threw it against the opposite wall. I yelled for somebody to turn off the music. I made a move to get to the box myself, and if Quake hadn't grabbed it, I probably would have bashed it against the bridge also.

"If I hear that song one more time, I swear, I'm going to climb up on that interstate and throw myself in front of a goddamn truck."

"Kyle, what's wrong?" Jennifer was taking hold of my arm, but I yanked it away.

"This is such bullshit!" I shouted at the top of my lungs.

Some guy in the shadows swore and told me to

keep my voice down. I didn't even bother to answer.

"We should have done this while she was alive!" I shouted just as loud as before. I wiped my hands all crazy over the mess I'd painted. "We should have come here and painted *We . . . love . . . you . . . Diana*—when she was alive. When she was alive and we weren't drunk. I can remember the first part—"

A truck door opened and slammed behind us. The engine started, and when I turned around, two red taillights were already heading down the road with a rumble of unmuffled exhaust.

"You got David all worked up," Shannon cried. "Now what's going to happen to him?"

"If he dies, we can paint a bridge for him, right? We've treated him like dog shit for years, but if he would just once get drunk and kill himself, he could have his own bridge."

Cindy said, "Listen, Kyle. We can't undo the past. We all feel terrible on account of Diana. Not just you. And anyway she wasn't drinking. If you don't want to do this, fine. Just go then. Diana doesn't belong to you."

"I'll go then," I said, and headed for my car. I heard Jennifer call after me. Then I heard Cindy shout, "Don't you go with him! Not when he's like this, you don't," and Jennifer say, "Let go of me."

It didn't take me long to get out of there.

Instantly there were headlights close behind me. Of course I knew they belonged to Quaker Oats.

The Salmon Falls Mini-Mart and Redemption Center is open twenty-four hours a day, but I'd never seen so many cars in the lot or so many people standing around past midnight. As mad as I was, I couldn't help but slow down to see what was up. Something was going on, I could tell, but I wouldn't be able to see what without getting out of my car. My feet were no sooner on the pavement than Quake was beside me.

"What's happening here?" he said, strangely out of breath.

"Beats me."

When we got to where we could see through the crowd, what we found was an awful mess of broken glass and torn-up boxboard all over the parking lot. I heard a guy say, "Here he comes again," just before David Logan shoved through the door of the Mini-Mart with three cases of beer, threw them all on the ground, and stomped them with his work boots. A woman in the Mini-Mart uniform came out behind him screaming, which some people in the crowd apparently found hilarious. David just moved her out of the way, not roughly, and went back into the store with her following behind still screaming.

We'd always talked about David as being slow, and that's what got me about this—how slow it was, almost like slow-motion in a movie. Later on, when people talked about "how David Logan trashed the Mini-Mart," they made it sound like he'd gone berserk, but Quake and I were there, and it wasn't like that. He just kept chugging along, as if all the beer in the coolers had gone bad and he'd been hired to haul it all outside and would be doing so for at least another hour for not a penny more than minimum wage. At one point there was this guy hanging on his back with a choke hold around his neck, and the night manager still screaming at him—he just kept moving till the guy dropped off. The sheriff arrived, and in the process of trying to get David under control, they both fell down together. David got himself up and headed back into the store with the sheriff and the other guy in pursuit. There was a terrible crash inside that sent Quake and me running for the door—it opened, and there was Dave with two six-packs in each hand. He nodded to us and then began breaking the bottles one at a time on the ground.

Quake and I eventually got pushed back into the bystanders when two state troopers arrived and together with the sheriff got David cuffed and face-down on the ground. We called out to him and shouted for the cops to take it easy, but they probably couldn't hear us in all the confusion. Some people, mostly kids but a few older than kids, were making a scramble every couple of minutes to snatch up the unbroken cans and bottles that were rolling around on the pavement.

I saw Reggie Barton and a few of his friends make a dash for some, and then Reg was at my elbow offering me a beer. I shook my head. He took a sip from his and gestured with the can toward the spectacle in front of us.

"Well, Kyle, with all respect to you and the Mahatma, I'd say the Lord just came to Ira County."

5

IT TOOK PUBLIC OPINION AT OUR HIGH SCHOOL ABOUT
two periods, say an hour and a half, to make up its
mind about David Logan and what he had done.

There seemed to be two main groups, what I'd
call the "sympathetic group" and the "offended
group," but they pretty much boiled down to the
same group, and they both relied a lot on the same
word, which was "stupid."

The opinion of the sympathetic group was that
there's just no coming between a retard and his grief.
Of course, this being the sympathetic group, most
people found nicer ways to say it. But that's what
they meant. Most of the teachers belonged to this
group, though I'm proud to say that Mrs. Cantor
didn't. She'd taken one of last year's yearbooks and
cut David's photo out and taped it to the outside of
the door to the resource room. She kept the door

closed all day, something she never did, though she was working with people on the inside as usual. I didn't stop by to talk to her, but I did stick my head in for just a second to say, "Like your door."

The offended group was the bigger of the two, or at least they had the most to say. For them it all came down to one simple fact: David Logan had disrespected the dead. The school was in mourning, Diana wasn't even in her grave, and David had spilled beer and thrown broken glass all over everyone's delicate feelings. In other words, the show was still going on, the hugs, the hysterics, the melodramatic entrances and exits—my own scene at the bridge being just one example—and David had had the gall to blow a fart in the back of the theater. All this when it had only been through the generosity of people like Diana that he'd been allowed to remain in the theater in the first place.

It was on that day that I learned something funny about grief, or mourning, or whatever you want to call it, which is that it works an awful lot like booze. Number one because people use it as an excuse to act like idiots, and number two because they can get awfully cranky if they think somebody's trying to take it away.

For the unusual opinion, see Quaker Oats—that was one reason why I was very eager to see him later that morning. We hadn't said much to each other the night before, just gotten into our separate cars and driven away, too stunned for much discussion. Now, though, I was needing a little oatmeal, so to speak, to get that potato-chip-and-chewing-gum taste out of my mouth.

"So have you thought any more about our man David?" I said.

We were at his locker, and I should have guessed he had some kind of pole up his rear by the way he kept looking up into the top compartment and fussing around with his books while he talked.

"It's pretty much just the last in a series, isn't it?" he said. "Probably not even the last."

"Series of what?"

"Misunderstandings. People taking . . . what our rebellion was trying to do and messing it all up."

"I don't think David gave one thought to our rebellion—"

"No, I'm sure he didn't give one thought. And Condor probably didn't give one thought when he grabbed Diana's container and tried to run away from the police, and the people who are saying we helped kill Diana probably are not giving one thought to what they're saying, but . . ."

He looked at me then.

"I *did* give it one thought, though. More than

one. I gave things a lot of thought. So did you. And so did Diana."

He sighed and closed his locker.

"As far as David goes, I'm sure he meant well, but it just wasn't very intelligent. Violence doesn't accomplish anything. I guess all I can say is that what he did makes me very sad."

"Well . . . I guess all I can say is fuck you, Quake."

I didn't hit him hard, just the back of my open hand against his chest. But I could feel the blow go through his whole body, and through mine.

6

ACCORDING TO MRS. CANTOR, DAVID "WAS VERY touched" when he heard that she'd invited me to join her on a visit to his house and that I wanted to go if it was all right with him. The mishap in the resource room and even our near fight after Diana's death were "in perspective now," she told me. She was going because David's lawyer from Legal Aid was meeting with him and his parents. She said there was a possibility that David might re-enroll in school on a home-tutorial basis and that a move like that could help his case if we could persuade him to make it.

"The lawyer thinks they're less likely to be too harsh on him if he's trying to get his diploma," she told me on the ride over.

"How harsh do you think they'll get?"

"I don't know, Kyle. But to be honest, it doesn't look all that promising. After some of the trouble you guys were in earlier this year, and after . . . the accident, there's a mood around for clamping down on teenagers. Some people are afraid that things have gotten out of control."

"Except, though, number one, David isn't a teenager, and number two, he had nothing to do with the trouble we were in or with the accident. He was nowhere near either."

"I know that," she said, still her old calm self. We were far enough up the narrow road that leads to David's house that grass was beginning to appear between the tire tracks. The dirt was pretty much dry by now but still rutted from mud season.

"But you know, Kyle, things aren't always as individualistic as you'd like, or as people your age often think they are. Everything we do sets wheels in motion that affect other people—and poor people especially."

Just then we heard something hard hit the underside of the car. The steering wheel jerked in Mrs. Cantor's hand.

"What the heck was that?" I turned around to look behind us.

"Let's pray it wasn't David," she said.

I'd been to David's house a number of times, but this was the first time I'd ever been inside it. Usually whenever I pulled into the dooryard, he'd be on the porch waiting or sliding through the front door with his jacket still off one arm. Since almost all the time we hung out together we spent hunting and fishing, it made sense that I never went in. When we'd start off, it was early and we didn't want to wake anybody up; when we got back, we were fishy enough or bloody enough that the dooryard seemed the best place for us.

So it seemed funny to step through the front door, at least for me. I had the feeling Mrs. Cantor might have been there before. She didn't have to ask where the bathroom was when she needed it. I didn't even know David's mother.

She was sitting on a kitchen chair next to David's father, who was in a saggy sort of easy chair that made him look shorter than her, though he wasn't. She had very straight hair, which was so carefully brushed and shiny and soft that I found myself staring at it, but when she talked I realized she didn't have a tooth in her head. She was what I guess you would have to call fat, but she'd put on this kind of nice flowery dress that was a little short for somebody her build but still looked like an outfit you'd put on to get dressed up. I thought later that she looked a lot like the inside of her house did, definitely poor yet very clean and pulled together.

I'd met David's father one or two times before, usually when he'd looked up from the engine of a car he was taking apart and a couple of times when he'd come over to supervise the butchering of a deer. His appearance was sort of the opposite of his wife's, in that on the one hand he did not look all that clean or pulled together, but on the other hand his body was in good shape, lean and muscular with that oiled kind of year-round tan guys have who live a ways off the main drag. He had on a hat with a picture of a rooster and some saying I couldn't read that well because the light was not all that bright and because when you looked too long at him he'd look right back in a You-got-a-problem? sort of way. He also had a thick dark beard and a thin braided ponytail down the back of his neck. He was in the middle of a conversation with the lawyer when we came through the door. David shook my hand as I passed by his chair— a younger brother had let us in—and then I sat on a small couch next to Mrs. Cantor.

"This trouble my boy is in is a great vexation to me, your honor."

"I'm just an attorney, sir. You don't need to call me 'your honor.'"

The lawyer was sitting on a hassock in front of

203

David's dad. He looked so young, I bet he'd have been happy if one or two people in the course of a day just called him mister.

"I realize that perfectly well, but this is exactly the point I want to make, which is that I have raised all four of my children to respect property and obey the law, which is why I call you 'your honor,' because as far as I'm concerned you show that kind of respect whether it be a judge, jury, or like yourself, it don't matter. One's just as important as another. And that's why my son's actions have made me so ashamed . . ."

Mr. Logan's voice got weak all of a sudden, so much that his wife began rubbing his shoulder.

". . . that when I go into town, I must wait until after dark . . . for fear they'll see my face."

Very quietly his wife said, "You always gone out at night, Ronnie."

He swatted her hand away from his shoulder like it was a fly. "Always gone out, yes! But not the way I do now, not so I don't go out during the day! See, she don't get it neither. I'm sorry, but I have to go outside for a smoke. I'm at the point I don't know what I'll do next."

I may be wrong, but I think I heard more than one sigh of relief when he got up from his chair. But Mrs. Logan just about begged him to stay, so we didn't get rid of him after all.

"All right, for my wife's sake, I will try to stay, but I can't guarantee how much more of this I can stand. I really can't."

The lawyer finally decided to make his move.

"Mr. Logan, your respect for the law is admirable, and I believe that David's upbringing is certainly evident in the fact that to my knowledge this is the first time David has ever run afoul of the law. Isn't that right, David?"

David looked away from us and nodded.

"But why should there be any time, that's what I want to know," his father cried out. "And not just mischief of a kind where boys will be boys, but an act of shameful destruction and wastefulness."

"Well, I think that's what we want to find out from David. David, can you tell me why you did what you did at the store?"

"Seems pretty obvious, don't it?"

That did not sit well with Dad.

"If it was so goddamn obvious you wouldn't be this far from a jail cell, would you? There wouldn't be all these people here, would there? You wouldn't have *charges* against you!" He leaned forward with his eyes almost squinted shut and pointed at his son. "You better smarten up. Or you're going to wish you had. Now answer this man's question. Why'd you do it?"

"'Cause Diana got killed!"

He said it so loud that even the old man sat back for a second. In what I guess was supposed to be a soothing voice but sounded a little like a whine, his mother said, "We told you a hundred times, David, Diana weren't drinking."

"He don't get it," Mr. Logan said, as if he were only talking to his wife, but I knew David could hear.

"The Man Upstairs gave my son a strong body, and he can do a man's work when he decides it's worth his while, but as far as the mind goes . . . well, you know all about that, Mrs. Cantor."

"There's nothing wrong with David's mind—" she began to say, but David interrupted her.

"I know she weren't drinking! Dumb as I am, I know that. But it killed her just the same. If that other fool weren't drunk, she'd be alive. And if I could make her alive again, I'd break every bottle of booze I could get my hands on and I wouldn't care if they shot me dead for doing it."

"We'd all do the same, son. If I thought I could bring that poor girl back to life, my lips would never touch an alcoholic beverage as long as I lived. But it won't bring her back to life no more'n what you did would stop anybody from drinking. If they taught you your history in school like they did when I was your age, they'd have told you about the Great

Probation. You ever heard of the Great Probation?"

David wouldn't bother to answer.

"They tried to make drinking illegal and it didn't work. They even had these holy rollers running around doing exactly what you did, and all it accomplished was it made people drink the more. They finally smartened up and put a stop to it. They seen it was a bad idea just like what come into that crazy head of yours was a bad idea. Everybody that's got sense knows it was a bad idea. Mr. Allen, you're a lawyer with probably more education than all the people in this room put together. Now you tell me if I'm wrong. Was the Great Probation a good idea or not?"

"It was pretty much a disaster, but—"

"Pretty much a disaster—there you go. Did you hear that, David? A disaster, which is what this household which I am the head of is heading toward right now. And all because you didn't know what every fool knows, which is that people have always right from Bible times to the present day drunk alcohol and they always will."

I wish David could have seen the look on Mrs. Cantor's face when he looked straight at his father and said, "In countries that have Buddha for their religion they don't drink, and in another one, too—Islam, I think they call it?"

I said, "Right"—my contribution for the evening. "Diana told me that."

"Well, isn't this sweet. Not only have we raised a jailbird, it looks like we've raised a Christly heathen too. Of course they don't drink! Your friend bother to tell you that in some of them countries they don't hardly *eat*? Some of them people is so backward they can't put seed in the ground unless we go over and show 'em how to do it. Buddha my backside. And as far as your Islams go, your friend wouldn't have played too much basketball in their league, I can tell you that. That bunch are notorious for abusing their women! And we're not just talking a kick in the old lady's keester now and again neither. We're talking real . . . mistreatment."

"But David, you've given us something important to think about." Mrs. Cantor smiled at Mrs. Logan, who at that moment seemed very distressed by the mistreatment of Islamic women. "It's the sign of an active mind," Mrs. Cantor added, nodding at David.

"He wants to do some thinking, he ought to think about passing his arithmetic. That'd be thinking enough for his active mind, I expect."

"This has been an interesting discussion," said the lawyer. "Right now, though, I think we better concentrate on giving David his day in court. By the way, David, just out of curiosity, how is your math going? Or how was it going?"

"Okay, I guess. Diana was helping me. She helped me more than anybody ever did."

I glanced out of the corner of my eye at Mrs. Cantor, but she was looking at David the same as before—like he was her favorite son.

"Well, I guess you're going to have to help yourself now," said Mr. Logan.

"I don't care about none of that no more."

"School's not your favorite thing in life, is it, David?" the lawyer asked.

David blew a stream of air against his lips. "If I had my way, I'd have never gone to school. It ain't ever done me no good and I ain't no good at it."

"There's a couple a understatements," said Guess Who.

"David, how would you feel if in court I asked you a few questions concerning school? In front of the judge."

"I might not know the answers. If you give me something to study—"

"No, no, not questions like that. It wouldn't be a test. I just would like to give the judge an opportunity to know how much you've struggled in school, your frustrations, the stress. Could I ask you about that, you think?"

David was looking down at his shoes. "I guess."

"Because I think that could be very helpful."

"You wouldn't have to say how old I was, would you? I'm a little older than some of the other seniors."

"We could possibly avoid that, although there probably wouldn't be any seniors there in court. Let's just worry for now about getting you as much off the hook as possible."

Mrs. Cantor was looking hard at the lawyer now. She seemed about to say something, but he spoke first.

"And Mrs. Cantor, if you'd be willing to come and say a few words about David, his studies and . . . his difficulties—"

"That will depend. David's program is protected by confidentiality."

"You don't need to worry about that," Mr. Logan said. "In view of some of the fines this boy is facing, I'd say confidentiality is a little more than this family can afford right now. Maybe some other time."

"Actually, Mr. Logan, I might request that you yourself, and maybe Mrs. Logan too, would agree to serve as witnesses when the time comes."

Mr. Logan seemed to consider this very seriously. "I'm not sure what I can offer to the case, your honor.

Like I said, we don't approve of our son's actions."

"No, of course not. I just thought that if the judge had a chance to see you in person, and hear about your upbringing of David, some of your thoughtful views on life, it might sway things in his favor."

"Well," said Mr. Logan, straightening up as best he could in his saggy chair, "I could certainly try. I'm not much of a talker. But I've never been one to hold back from helping my children."

When the lawyer asked if he could speak to David's parents and teacher alone, I was suspicious, but David couldn't get out of the house fast enough. I decided to go with him. It was almost dark now, with a light-blue border over the mountains and the first stars in the sky. Four or five of the Logan dogs were milling around the dooryard, and David stooped to pat and scratch each one on his way to his truck. He threw down the tailgate and sat on it. When he saw me hesitate, he said, "There's room for you."

Right then I wanted to tell him how sorry I was for what had happened in the resource room that day and for just about everything that had happened since. Instead I just sat still next to him. We faced the house, which looked black in the twilight, and watched his parents and the lawyer through the lit-up curtains. We couldn't see Mrs. Cantor.

"So what do you think of all this, David?" I said at last.

"Not much," he said.

"What do you think will— Whoa!"

An enormous owl swooped low and skimmed the dust in the dooryard. We couldn't see if it caught anything.

"That bird's been around here for the past two weeks. If we had puppies or chickens outside, it'd be a big problem."

In a minute I tried again. "You think your lawyer knows what he's doing?"

"Oh yeah. He knows what he's going to be doing too."

He reached behind him in the truck bed and threw a wood chip toward the house.

"He's going to try to save my ass by proving I was too dumb to know better."

I didn't know what to say.

"If that don't work, he'll get my whole family up there so the judge can see how dumb the bunch of us is."

"You don't have to go along with it, Dave."

"I don't, huh? What's your idea then? What do you think I should do? Prove I'm smart?"

7

I GUESS THAT DAVID'S DAY IN COURT WAS ONE OF THOSE events meant to be seen by only a few people, although later on other people will say that if they'd known about it, they would have shown up. What they really mean is that if they'd known what was going to happen, they wouldn't have missed it for the world.

Besides a handful of people I didn't recognize, there were just a few of us from David's family or from school. His parents were there, of course, and Mrs. Cantor, and of all people Diana's father. I was also surprised to see Mr. Keller, the big mouth from the funeral. The same reporter who'd shown up late at our civil disobedience was early today. I came with my mother, as did Quake with his. Quake's father joined them a few minutes after things had gotten started. They sat about as far front as we did, on the opposite side of the courtroom from us. There were a few other students I recognized, though we didn't have any classes together. Shannon didn't come. Neither did Jennifer, though she told me to wish David good luck from her.

I suppose it made sense that the courtroom looked different to David than to me. I know it did because when we saw each other for a few minutes out in the hallway, he said, "Why in hell are there so many people in there? It ain't nobody's business but mine."

It was the only time I ever saw him look afraid. I think he was more afraid of being in front of that handful of people than he was of any sentence he might receive. It made me realize that maybe for him the hardest thing about trashing the Mini-Mart was having people watch.

That's not to say David had no fear of punishment. I could have cried when he leaned down to me just as he was being called in and said, "If they lock me up, would you come see me?"

"They're not going to lock you up" was all I had time to say. I wish I'd just said, "Yes."

As I remember it, Quake got up to leave at around the same time as Mr. Logan was saying something about "The Great Probation" and the judge said, "You mean Prohibition, don't you?" Somebody laughed under their breath. To tell you the truth, Mr. Logan wasn't in as good a form as he'd been in a few nights ago, but the lawyer was doing everything he could to warm him up. He had at least managed to get Logan to say a thing or two about his son's mind.

I got up as soon as Quake did. I think it was a combination of having seen one too many people bolt up and leave over the past several weeks and my fear for David and the fact that I was still pretty disgusted with Quake that made me chase after him like I did. Even though I felt ashamed for hitting him at his locker, I think that if I could have caught him I would have dragged him back into that court by his hair. I wanted him to see for once in his life that reality isn't just a bunch of smart people with good ideas making everything into some kind of game.

He'd apparently broken into a sprint as soon as he got through the doors. I tore off after him.

The courthouse in Angle Junction sits up on a little hill overlooking the upper part of Main Street. He was halfway down the long lawn before I was close enough to be sure he could hear me.

"It gets better," I shouted after him, still running. He looked over his shoulder and seemed to slow down for a minute. I was soon even with him.

"Wait till you see what they're going to do with David."

He started to speed up again.

"Don't you want to see . . . his senseless violence . . . get punished?"

I stopped running, catching my breath in big swallows, and watched him tear across the street. I remember thinking, he's the same kid he was in graded school—still running away from a fight.

I would have turned then and hustled back to the court if I hadn't seen him run straight to the market on the corner. In less than a minute he was out again, in a sudden flash of white shirt, with his sport jacket draped over his arm. He crossed the street and began running toward me. A man in a red butcher's apron came out of the store waving his arms and shouting. Quake turned several times and shouted something over his shoulder that I couldn't hear until he repeated it about fifty feet away.

"Keep the change," he called, though by this time the man had gone back into the store. I could tell that Quake wasn't going to stop once he reached me, so I turned and got in position to start running back with him.

"What are you doing?" I said, once we were running side by side again. He was winded some from running uphill and shouting to the storekeeper, but he was also wearing a grin I hadn't seen on his face since before Diana died.

"Making a beer run, dude."

Still running, he pulled his sport jacket farther up his arm to reveal a six-pack of beer bottles. "Here, have a brewski."

I almost didn't catch it.

"What the hell am I supposed to do with this?"

"You'll know when the time comes."

He came to a stop in front of a garbage can just below the court steps. He clamped the six-pack between his knees and put his jacket back on. Then he stuck a bottle into each of the inside breast pockets of his jacket.

"You look like you got tits," I said.

"I'm gonna need 'em."

He threw the rest of the six-pack into the garbage can. Things were happening so fast that if I'd suddenly seen a spaceship overhead and if a ladder had come down for Quake, I might not have been too surprised. I had the strange sense that he was about to go away. He was tucking my bottle into the waist of my pants.

"Quake, I feel real bad I hit you that day."

He gave my cheek a couple of light slaps. He was still panting, still grinning. "I know that," he said, like it was so obvious that any fool would know the same thing. "You're a good man, Kyle."

He seemed to believe that was obvious too.

• • •

"David, you are not at this time officially enrolled in school, is that correct?"

"No, sir."

"Can you speak up a little, please?"

Even from the back of the court, I could see him swallow before repeating his answer. I was a couple of rows behind my mother now, though Quake had rejoined his parents on the other side of the room. He had told the officer at the door that we'd gone outside to pray.

"When did you drop out, David?"

"A few weeks ago, I guess."

"And you were a senior at the time, is that correct?"

David nodded.

"Please say yes or no, David. We have to record your answer."

"Yes."

"And you were not far from receiving your diploma?"

"If I would've passed everything, yeah."

"And what was everything?"

"A math and an English."

"Now can you explain for the court why you dropped out? What made you decide to leave school when you were almost in sight of your diploma?"

"I guess . . . when Diana LaValley got killed . . . I felt like there weren't no point."

"Diana was your tutor, wasn't she?"

"Yes, sir."

"Now, David"—here the lawyer stepped out from behind the table that had his notes on it—"why was Diana tutoring you?"

"She was just like that. She would've helped anybody."

I wondered if the lawyer had any idea that the large man wiping his eyes was Diana's father. Probably if he had, he wouldn't have passed a little smile to the judge.

"Did you like Diana, David?"

"Never met anybody that didn't."

"But as a young man, I mean . . . was Diana the kind of girl you would have liked to go out with?"

"I'm not really sure what you're asking me."

"Well, was she—"

"We were friends. And she was helping me out. I liked her 'cause she was a nice person, that's all. Plus I think my best buddy was a little sweet on her, and I never would've done nothing to get in his way."

My mother turned around, but I just stared at my lap. I knew her face would look about the same as mine.

"What was Diana tutoring you in, David?"

"Math."

"Do you like math? Is math a subject you enjoy?"

"No way."

A little bit of nervous laughter broke out in the court. It seemed to embarrass David—he would never suppose that the people were laughing because they hadn't enjoyed math either.

"What's your best subject, David?"

"I don't know if I have a best subject. I did pretty good in ag shop there, when I had that."

"What kinds of things was Diana tutoring you in? You said math, but can you be more specific?"

"I don't know, just regular math."

"Mm-hm. David . . . how old are you right now?"

For the first time, David took his eyes off the lawyer.

"David, will you please tell us—"

"I want to ask you something for a minute, if you don't mind," David said. "Is that guy writing over there from the newspaper?"

"He may be, but that's not important to us right now. David, will you look at me, please?"

David did, but then he said, "I just wanted to know where my answers was going, like as far as my confidentiality goes and like that."

Now he was looking desperately toward Mrs. Cantor. His father exhaled between his teeth and made a big show of folding his arms over his chest.

"All we want to know, David, is how old you are. You're a senior in high school, or you were until a few weeks ago, and we'd like to know your age."

"Your honor, I believe I have something to contribute to the court."

The sound of a new voice sucked every other sound out of the place. Of course I knew right where to look. Quaker Oats was on his feet.

"That may well be," the judge said after looking him up and down. "And there are proper procedures for doing so."

"I apologize for the interruption, but I won't take more than a minute of the court's time. I just wanted you to know that I am a senior at the same high school David goes to, I'm seventeen years old, and I have a four-point-oh grade point average."

"I'm very glad to hear it," said the judge. "Officer Johnson—"

"I also have SAT scores that total more than fourteen hundred and I'll be a freshman at Swarthmore College next fall on a full scholarship."

As the officer moved toward Quake, he stepped out of his row and began sidling down another. The officer began to move faster, and a murmur went through the room. I heard my mother say out loud, "What is he doing?"

"The only other thing you need to know about me, your honor, is that I destroy beer bottles as a form of social protest."

He managed to get both bottles out of his jacket and to smash one and then the other on the back of the bench in front of him. The noise was such a shock that even the officer stopped dead for a second. Before Quake shattered the second bottle, which was just before the officer grabbed him, he called out in a loud voice, "But David Logan had the brains to think of it first!"

I was on my feet; so was everyone else. Quake was standing calmly now, with the officer holding both of my friend's hands behind his back. Even on my side of the room I picked up a whiff of beer, such a strange smell in this place. The judge was banging his gavel and ordering everybody out of the court-room. I was so paralyzed by what had just happened that I didn't even remember I was holding a bottle of beer in my hand. It was Mrs. Cantor who noticed it, passing by me on her way out of court.

"You better do something with that," she said.

8

THE JUDGE CALLED FOR A THIRTY-MINUTE RECESS,
during which he talked to Quake and David in his
chambers. After about twenty minutes a woman
came outside the building, where we were all waiting, and said he wanted to talk to me.

David and Quake were both sentenced to two
hundred and forty hours of community service, one
hundred and twenty of which were to be spent working at the Salmon Falls Mini-Mart as a form of resti-
tution. They both had to write letters of apology,
David to the Mini-Mart and Quake to the court.

The shocker came when the judge also sentenced Quake to three days in the county jail. He
said that he believed Quake's motives were of the
highest sort, but that was all the more reason "to
uphold the sanctity of the law." He said society
must never believe that having good intentions is

sufficient justification for doing otherwise.

"Sometimes laws are broken in order that society may improve, and it may be that this young gentleman will make a career of such disobedience. If so I wish him well. I also wish him to learn that such actions have a very real personal cost."

Quake's parents both stood up at that point, and his mother found the voice to say, "You had better confine me also then, because if our son should suffer any injury whatsoever in jail, I swear to you—"

The judge cut her off.

"Madam, before you swear to anything that will lead you or me to have any regrets, let me promise you that your son will have no cellmates and will be held under the strictest and most benevolent supervision. This court is adjourned."

I doubt Quake would have had much trouble at that point, in jail or out, because word was soon passing like wildfire through the redneck grapevine that anybody who laid a hand on "the Quaker boy" was likely to have a bad accident involving a hand. I doubt many people really understood what Quake had tried to do. All they knew was that he had committed an outrage in a court of law, that it was done on behalf of a friend, and that it involved beer. Two out of three would have been enough to make him a local hero.

In fact, it was not unusual at parties throughout that summer and even into the following fall for somebody to break a full bottle of beer against a rock or a guardrail and say, "This one's for Quaker Oats."

So my friend, who had been a pacifist since kindergarten and who claimed to have called himself an environmentalist since about third grade, now found himself protected by threats of murder and mayhem and honored across the county by acts that nobody would call recycling. It was, as Mr. Logan would have put it, "a great vexation" to him. I would just pat him on the back now and then and say, "Politics as usual, Quake."

Condor Christy got out of the hospital sometime in late May with a few strange facial mannerisms and a better than sixty-percent chance of regaining the full use of his legs. They wheeled him up for his blank diploma, and the senior class gave him a standing ovation. He also got the first Diana LaValley Memorial Scholarship, which some people said should have gone to me, but I didn't need it. What would I have done with that?

Condor moved back to California as soon as his makeup work was done or waived. I dropped by to see him off. I told myself I was doing it for Diana. After we'd gotten him into the special van his mother had leased, and after his little sister had given me a hug and climbed in beside him, Mrs. Christy closed the side door and thanked me for my "support." She wasn't being sarcastic, but she probably had a right to be. True, I had dropped by their house a couple of times with Jennifer, and one time on my own when I'd gotten roped into bringing Condor his final exam reviews, but I'd hardly given her son so much as a smile since the accident.

Then his mother said, "I thought we had problems in California, but as far as I'm concerned, the real problems started here. I'm glad we're leaving. I hate this place and everything about it."

Maybe it was because I didn't appreciate that remark that I had the nerve to say, "California couldn't have been that great either."

"No, it wasn't," she said. "Not at the end. It might have been. . . ."

"So what happened in California, if you don't mind me asking?"

I'd have walked to California barefoot not to hear the way she laughed right then.

"What happened? Something unforgivable! My son fell in love for the first time in his life."

The way she was bugging out her eyes at me, I knew I was being dared to ask the next question. Was this woman about to blame me because the second time her kid fell in love hadn't worked out so hot either?

"So . . . what was wrong with that?" I said.

"You'll have to ask the lowlifes he went to school with. The other kid was smaller, so Condor didn't even get the worst of it. I guess poor Miss LaValley was supposed to be my son's proof that he was normal. Except . . . he doesn't look too normal now, does he?"

That was it. I couldn't stand another minute of the look on her face. I went back around to the side of the van and pulled the side door open. I gave Condor another good-bye handshake, one of those homey jobs like he used to give me in the hall, and I gave him a hug too. And then I said what he'd said to me that day in the hospital: "We were her guys."

And we were, weren't we? Two screwups, both afraid to show all their cards. Anyway, when Condor and his family finally hit the road, I let my bitterness do the same.

You could probably write a whole book just on the summer that Quake and David spent working off their sentence at the Mini-Mart and all the games Quake invented to pass the time—like Broom Zoom and Guess the Gallons—and the day he got David to wear a gigantic fake beard to work, not to mention the night that David roped Quake into driving in a demolition derby. I'll always wonder if some of the fun they had was their way of putting the long arm of the law into a sling or if the judge had intended a partnership like theirs all along. I know that at first I was really pissed about their sentence, way more than either of them was, though I did pitch in now and then with some of the community service work. The way I saw it was like this: Blood all over the highway was just one of those unfortunate teenage tragedies that the world was prepared to tolerate now and again, but private property trashed all over the pavement, even if it was an honest protest against the blood, well, we just couldn't put up with that.

In the end, though, even I had to admit that there was something unfair in the Salmon Falls Mini-Mart getting trashed on behalf of Diana, because Marcel Fontaine, the owner, was always known far and wide as a real hardass when it came to carding minors. He wasn't a hardass to work for, though. Quake said that he'd rag on the two of them now and again if their antics got too wild, but that he never once brought up the reason that the two of them had to be there.

On their last night, when I went to pick them up for a little "emancipation celebration," Fontaine surprised us all by offering David a full-time job at well over the minimum wage. David could work part-time at the Mini-Mart and part-time at Fontaine's other operations, which included construction and livestock sales. The only condition was that David get his high school diploma. It was David who brought up the past.

"I can't see you doing this after what I done."

"Listen," Fontaine said. "Everybody for a hundred miles who can read a newspaper knows what a dangerous character you are when you're riled up about something. What better security system could I buy than that?"

I don't think I ever mentioned that David never has any difficulty looking a gift horse in the mouth or sticking his foot into his own. He told Fontaine straight out that he'd take the job and work hard at it, but he'd have to have two weeks off in November for deer season, that he'd never in his life worked those two weeks, nor his father before him, and that he never would even if it meant he'd be a bum till he died.

At that point I was peeking at Fontaine from under my eyelids with my head sort of bowed, and Quake was looking over at the gas pumps with an expression on his face that suggested he was about to try to distract us by whistling a tune.

David lowered his voice and concluded, "So if you don't want to hire me, no hard feelings."

"Hire you!" Fontaine said, so loud I saw Quake wince. "Hire you!" he said again just as loud. "After that little tirade, my boy, I just might have to adopt you."

They walked back into the store with Fontaine asking what David thought was the greatest deer rifle ever made and warning him to think hard before he answered. Dave looked over his shoulder to tell us he'd be back out in a minute. I realized then that he might not be doing all his hunting with me that fall. Everybody was on the move. Even Jennifer Burch, who would leave for college the week after Quake did, had written me a little note saying it was time we thought of each other as just friends.

PART 4

MY FIRST DAY AT NORTHEAST PLASTICS, WHERE I WENT to work about a week after Quake left for college, was a lot like the hard frost that hit the vegetable gardens of Ira County at about the same time. A cold shriveling slap of reality. I don't mean that working at the mill was any kind of a big shock in itself. As I've said, I used to visit my father there on his breaks, and my mother had been working in the office since before I was born, so the place was practically like home.

What I mean is that as long as I was a high school kid telling my teachers or my father or even my friends that I wasn't going to college or leaving Salmon Falls, at least not right away, and that I just might work as a jughead for the rest of my life, I could count on a certain reaction. And to be honest, I think I liked that reaction. It was part of what gave me my basic Kyle quality, what made it impossible to pin me down with any one label. Drinks with the preps, hunts with the chucks, rides off into the sunset—or I guess in this case it would be the sunrise—with his lunch pail and the first shift whistle blowing like the bugle at Custer's last stand. That's Kyle for you.

But when I actually walked through the factory gates, it wasn't anything special—not for me, not for anybody, especially not for anybody who'd been humping on the line year in and year out. "This is Kyle, and this is his first day here. He's training on first shift and then he'll be moving to second." Noted. It was probably something like being the neighborhood badass where you have a certain reputation you can count on, but then all of a sudden you're just another loser carrying his folded-up clothes to his jail cell. There's where you punch your card, son, there's where you store your gloves and goggles, there's where you go to the john. Any questions?

Maybe I was just missing Quake, and that's why I felt so bummed out.

My father dropped by my department later in the day, and he did his best not to be too sarcastic when he said, "How you liking it?" Of course he wanted to say more. He wasn't going to rag on me, though, because we had made a deal over the summer that he wouldn't push college for a whole year if I promised, after the year was up, to give college some serious thought.

Well, I was giving it serious thought by about lunchtime. I was even wondering if my father had been right about me all along, that I was a spiteful little fool who did everything for spite. Maybe that was the whole reason I was standing there watching this big steel bitch of a machine dropping quadruplets of hot plastic jugs when I could have been asking some tall blonde with a pierced belly button how to find the campus bookstore.

But that's not true, not completely. It's funny, but sometimes when you finally admit a thing about yourself, a not-so-wonderful thing, you're able to see all the ways that thing doesn't come close to describing who you are. Back when you were refusing to admit it, you worried it might be the whole truth and nothing but the truth about yourself, but then you say, "Okay, so it's true!" and discover it's only part true. I hadn't stayed in Salmon Falls out of spite, or even out of grief over Diana getting killed, like some people were saying, though both those things might have been partial reasons. I stayed in town because of something that can feel like spite or grief, the way it eats at you and makes you rebel against other people's expectations, but is something different, and I would have to say it is love. Maybe after all that's happened, including losing somebody before I had the chance to really show her how I felt, I can admit that to myself too. Maybe I've grown up enough to admit that I love Ira County and the people in Ira County and the woods and streams thereabouts and that I couldn't just walk away from them, at least not for a while. And maybe, who knows, that's my special talent, like basketball was for Diana or hunting is for David or just about anything that takes a brain is for Quake: that when I love something, I love it very much.

You can laugh if you want. When all this stuff first came to me, I almost started laughing too. They had put me in one of the "designated noisy areas" at the plant, which means you're supposed to wear ear protection, though some of the old-timers are too deaf by now to care. I looked over at the machine next to mine, and there was this guy in an orange headset, like a pair of hard plastic earmuffs, singing to himself and bopping around like a redneck DJ. And right away my mind went back to that day with David Logan in the resource room, when his head-phones had disconnected and his Transylvanian math music had started blaring all over the place. I'd felt then as if I were seeing David for the first time in my life, all his pain and all his pride, and I asked myself, there in the mill, what do you call a weird feeling like I had that day? The only answer I could come up with was love.

And for the whole rest of the morning it was like all I saw were men and women wearing David's headphones.

That night at supper my mother took a bottle of beer with my name written on the label out of the refrigerator and set it by my plate. I started to explain that I hadn't been drinking in the house behind her back, but she put her fingers over my mouth and said, "Maybe we need to change the rules now that you're a working guy. You earned this."

I turned for a second to watch her rummage in the drawer for an opener, then looked back at the bottle. Leave it to Quake to have bought "a premium brand" without a twist-off cap, even if he was only going to smash it to pieces. It was the same bottle he'd handed to me outside the county courthouse. Mom must have found it in my room and chilled it for me.

If I was superstitious at all, I'd have believed that it was my fate to drink a beer that day, because this was actually the second time in two hours that somebody had offered me one, and with almost the exact same words as my mom's. When I was walking home after work, three guys waved me over to a pickup parked across from Frenchy's Market. One of them turned out to be my dad.

As soon as I got there, I saw that the other two were drinking. One of them broke me off a can, and he must have given my father an Is-this-okay? look because Dad said, "It don't bother me none. He can make up his own mind."

The other guy said, "I just thought with you being on the wagon . . . but hell, he deserves a drink, putting in his first day in that pisshole."

"He deserves something," my father said.

It was fairly easy then to shake my head and say, "Maybe later." Nobody was going to ask me what I meant by later.

But here with my mom standing next to my chair and giving me the man-of-the-house treatment, it was a little harder to put my hand over the bottle top. That's what I did, though.

"I'm saving this. Thanks just the same."

Mom stepped back to where I could see her face and she could see mine.

"What are you saving it for?"

"My birthday."

"That ain't for another couple months."

"Try years. I'm saving it for when I turn twenty-one."

Another woman couldn't have resisted asking her kid if he was talking about this beer or all beer, but my mom didn't ask because she isn't nosey like that and because I think she already knew the answer. She went to put the bottle back in the refrigerator, but she set it on the counter instead.

"No sense having it take up room in the fridge."

I let out a deep breath and took in another.

"If I go away to college next year . . . I can take it with me. Get it out of your way."

Her mouth smiled, but her eyes were wet.

"Your roommates'll just drink it up on you. I better keep it here."

I thought she was going to her purse for a tissue, but she came back with her cigarettes. She folded the pack into my fingers and squeezed my hand.

"You keep these for me," she said.

She kissed me on the cheek. And then we just ate.

I didn't tell Mom all my plans for that bottle of beer or what I planned to study in college, though I'd been thinking about the one ever since Mrs. Cantor had passed me in the courtroom and said, "You better do something with that," and I'd been thinking about the other for a while too. I'd certainly thought about it that first day at the mill, and I was thinking about it now as I opened up the book that had been collecting dust all summer on my dresser top. It was called *Breaking the Thread: The Story of the Paterson Silk Mill Strike of 1913*, and for the first time I intended to get past reading what was handwritten inside the cover:

To my working-class hero: Don't work too hard, don't drink too much, and don't sell yourself short.
> *With love and best wishes on your graduation,*
> *Rachel Cantor*
P.S. My grandmother is the one with the dark frizzy hair, third from the right, on page 62.

Damned if she didn't look just like Mrs. Cantor, only younger, and more old-fashioned in her long white dress and, in spite of everything that must have been going on in Paterson, New Jersey, in 1913, a lot less worried and worn out.

Anyway, Mrs. Cantor will certainly be one of the people I invite to my twenty-first birthday party, along with Michael and Hermeena and David and his new woman, who he tells me will soon be his wife "because it's the right thing" seeing as she's due to carry on the Logan line in about another seven or eight months. Go on, shake your head, I shook mine too, but I'll bet you my next three paychecks that David will turn out to be a better husband and father than any man he's ever known.

I'll drink to it, in fact, because that's what I've decided to do with that bottle of beer, my only souvenir from our short-lived rebellion and from David's unforgettable day in court. I'm going to drink toasts to all the people I love and even to some of the people they love, to David and his new family, to Mrs. Cantor and her grandmother, and you can bet I'll be drinking to my mother and father, whether they manage to stay on their wagons or not.

I will also drink to Diana LaValley. She seemed to come back to me that first day at work, right when I was feeling the most down, and she has been with me ever since. I don't mean as a ghost, which is something I don't believe in, but that I can see her standing there in her basketball uniform telling me, like she used to tell the shortest freshman on her team, to step up to the line and take my foul shots because sometimes they're all you get for the foul things that happen in your life. They belong to you, and you should just take them and let everybody else worry about whether or not they go in. I will drink a good toast to Diana.

And then with my glass still more than half full, and hoping my life is too, I will drink to Quaker Oats, wherever he may be. Only I will call him Christopher, because that is his name.